To Reneé

Thanks

This Can't Be Love!

A novel with poetry for the soul

by

Patricia Goins

Bloomington, IN   Milton Keynes, UK

authorHOUSE®

AuthorHouse™
1663 Liberty Drive, Suite 200
Bloomington, IN 47403
www.authorhouse.com
Phone: 1-800-839-8640

AuthorHouse™ UK Ltd.
500 Avebury Boulevard
Central Milton Keynes, MK9 2BE
www.authorhouse.co.uk
Phone: 08001974150

First published by AuthorHouse 8/11/2006
ISBN: 1-4259-5149-X (sc)

Printed in the United States of America
Bloomington, Indiana

This book is printed on acid-free paper.

TABLE OF CONTENTS

PART I.. ix

   PRELUDE.. xi

   CHAPTER 1 1

   CHAPTER 2 7

PART II.. 13

   CHAPTER 3 15

   CHAPTER 4 24

   CHAPTER 5 35

   CHAPTER 6 43

   CHAPTER 7 50

   CHAPTER 8 55

   CHAPTER 9 64

PART III... 73

   CHAPTER 10 75

   CHAPTER 11 81

   CHAPTER 12 87

   CHAPTER 13 93

PART IV... 101

   CHAPTER 14 103

   CHAPTER 15 112

   CHAPTER 16 121

CHAPTER 17 127

CHAPTER 18 136

CHAPTER 19 147

PART V 153

CHAPTER 20 155

CHAPTER 21 162

CHAPTER 22 170

CHAPTER 23 175

PART VI 183

CHAPTER 23 185

CHAPTER 24 194

WORDS FROM THE AUTHOR 196

ESSENCE THE POETRY OF LIFE 199

LOVE OR LUST... 200

SECRETS 202

I dedicate this book to my Lord and Savior Jesus Christ, I love you and I give you all the Honor and Praise for you are the most high. I decided to take a step of faith and trust you. Just as your word promised, my latter has been better than my past.

To my children, Aaron, Ebony, Isaiah, and Joshua you are the loves of my life.

To Safe Haven, thank you for providing me with shelter during my storms.

To Faith Deliverance International World Ministries, Apostle Mary Winfrey, 4185 Glenwood Rd, Decatur, Ga. I want to say thank you for providing me with spiritual guidance. Anyone searching for a church family to call their own, I invite you to visit FDIWM, your life will never be the same.

To Nicole Goins-Turner, Monique Bates, Marie Cox, and Sudie Delbridge, thank you for encouraging me to take a step of faith and go after my dreams.

Last but not least, to my Grandmother Kathleen Goins, thank you for saving me.

CHILD ABUSE

PART I

Somewhere a little girl dreams of being a star.

Somewhere a little boy dreams of racing cars.

Somewhere a little girl is being abused.

Somewhere a little boy is being misused.

Children are a blessing sent from above.

Entrusted in their parents care to be treated with love.

A child does not stay a child for long.

God has a purpose for those little ones.

We must protect our daughters and sons.

PRELUDE

If I were completely honest with myself, I would admit that the abuse started long before I met my husband. My first experience with domestic violence started when I lived with my father and stepmother. I was only seven years' old living at 1969 Livingston Avenue in Columbus, Ohio...

CHAPTER 1

I ran home from school as usual, I stopped near the front of my building and looked at the papers I was holding in my hand. I missed four words on my spelling test. Helen warned me that if I missed even one word on the test that she was going to make me write all the spelling words fifty times each. I tore the spelling test off my graded homework packet, and threw it down the gutter. When I walked in the back door, my stepmother was sitting at the kitchen table.

"Let me see your homework packet." She said with a look of disgust on her face.

Sometimes I could feel how much she hated me just by the way she looked at me. I handed her the packet.

"Where is the spelling test?" Helen yelled as she flipped through the pages.

"I lost it," I stuttered.

"What have I told you about lying to me Karen?"

"Not to tell lies because you hate liars."

"Take your ass to your room!" She yelled shoving me toward my bedroom. My heart started beating fast and my palms started sweating. I walked slowly to my room and sat down on my bed waiting for her. Helen walked into my room a few minutes later holding a ping-pong paddle in her hand.

"Take off your pants and lay across the bed."

"Yes ma'am." I did as I was told, lying across the bed on my stomach.

"I hate liars!" Helen screamed with each lick.

"I'm sorry, I won't lie anymore!" I screamed. I knew better than to get off the bed, if I tried to run she would hurt me even worse. When she finally got tired, she stopped and left the room, slamming my bedroom door behind her. I just laid there for a while and cried. I was too sore to move. I felt like my buttocks were on fire.

The next day when I went to school, I could hardly sit down in my chair. When I returned home from school that afternoon, I was surprised to see my father's car in the parking lot, he had not been home in three days. I was sitting on my bed reading a book when my father walked into my room. Helen had left to go to the grocery store.

"Helen told me how bad you have been acting. She said that you have started lying again, you are going to get a whipping. I want you to take down your panties and lay on the bed." I thought he was going to pull out a paddle as Helen had done the day before. I did not think I could stand another beating with the paddle, but instead of pulling out a paddle, he unzipped his pants, pulled them down and got on top of me. I felt something soft touching me in my private area. I really did not understand what my father was doing, but I was glad he had not pulled out Helen's paddle. He suddenly stood up, pulled his pants back up, pulled off his belt, and began hitting me with it. After hitting me two or three times with the belt, he stopped.

"If Helen asks you what happened you tell her that I whipped you, do not tell her anything else because that's all that happened," he said as he walked out of my room. I cried as I pulled my underwear and my pants back up.

That was the first of many times that my father molested me while I lived with him and his wife, he would return home after being gone for a few days and go straight to the basement.

"Helen, send Karen downstairs!" I would hear him yell, I always knew what was in store for me once I got to the basement. He would have me lock the door, and then tell me to take my panties off and lie on the floor, he was never able to penetrate me because his manhood was always too soft. I knew that what my father was doing to me was wrong. Helen must have known what was going on in the basement because she started being very cruel and brutal toward me.

"Karen, get your ass in here and eat this food!" Helen yelled from the kitchen one day, I had been feeling sick all day and really did not want to eat. However, I knew what would happen if I did not obey her. I walked slowly to the kitchen table and sat down, just the sight of food was making me nauseated. I attempted to put some peas in my mouth and immediately started gagging.

"You had better not throw up, or I will make you eat it!" She screamed. She was standing behind me at the stove boiling some water. I tried my best not to throw up, I forced the food down my throat. Unfortunately, my stomach did not care about Helens demands. I immediately started vomiting, all of the food I had eaten during the day came up and flooded the plate. She turned around toward me, "I told you not to throw up!" Helen yelled as she smashed my face into the plate.

"Eat it!" She yelled. I began crying and snorting, I could feel the vomit entering my nose and almost suffocating me, she suddenly released my head, turned around, grabbed the hot kettle of boiling hot water off the stove, and poured it on my arm. I screamed as I felt the searing pain and watched the skin on my arm begin to bubble. She grabbed me by my hair and pulled me up from the table, pushing me toward my bedroom. I ran into the room and cried as I held my injured arm in my hand. Later that evening, Helen entered my room, took one look at the horrible wound on my arm and left out. She returned with butter and smeared it over my arm.

Neither Helen nor my father took me to the emergency room.

Helen would beat me with anything she could find. It was as if she enjoyed seeing me bleed and cry in pain. She once hit me in the back of the head with a crowbar.

Another time she got so angry with me, she went to the kitchen, picked up a butcher knife and stabbed me in my foot. I never could understand why she hated me so much.

The more I tried to be good, the worse the beatings got. At some point Helen began beating me with jumper cables, she would have me stand next to the bed while she beat me in the exact same spot, repeatedly until blood started pouring down my leg.

One summer she did so much damage to my right leg that I spent the entire summer learning how to walk again.

"Go down to the basement and count all of your toys," Helen said one Saturday afternoon.

"You better not miss count or you know what will happen," she had the look of Satan on her face.

I walked down the stairs as I was told, poured the big box of toys on the floor, and began counting. When I was finished, I walked back up the stairs and knocked on the door.

"What!" She yelled from the other side of the door.

"I'm finished counting mommy." I said in a low timid voice. During the course of my time living with Helen she began making me call her mommy. She slowly opened the door and gave me a cold stare.

"How many did you count?"

"Eighty-five," I answered meekly.

"You had better be right or you are going to get it," she said as she walked toward the basement steps, I walked to my bedroom and sat on the bed.

"I know I counted eighty-five," I said aloud as I nervously held my hands. I could feel my palms getting moist, she came back in the room with the jumper cables in her hand.

"You were wrong. There was ninety, drop your pants," Helen said in a low voice. After the beating I dropped to my knees holding my thigh as blood gushed out of my reopened wound, I began crying harder than I had ever cried before.

I was so scared of Helen; my father was never around to save me. Whenever he came home, he acted as if he didn't know she was torturing me, all he did was continue to take me on trips to the basement. Grandma Ellis and my mother were dead.

I did not have anyone to protect me. I began praying every morning before I got out of bed.

"Thank you God, for waking me up this morning, please protect me, and please forgive me for being bad." I would whisper.

I ran away from home twice. Each time the police found me, they returned me to my father, Helen would punish me for running away by locking me in my bedroom, and only feeding me rice and water.

The teachers at my school must have noticed how horrible I looked and knew that something was wrong. The school nurse called me into her office one afternoon. She was an older white woman. I liked her because she was always nice to me.

"Karen, are you being mistreated at home?" She asked.

"No Ms. Thompson," I answered. I knew that if I told on Helen and my father, I would get a beating if they found out.

"The gym teacher said that you have a very big scar on your leg, can I see it?"

She asked. I lowered my pants and allowed her to see the ugly scar I had received from being beat with the jumper cables, when she saw the old wound she gasped.

"Oh my Karen, how did that happen?" She asked as she lightly ran her fingers over the large scar.

"I fell on some glass while I was riding my bike." I lied. Trying not to look at her face, I figured that if I looked into her eyes she would know I was lying.

"Okay Karen, you can pull your pants up and go back to class."

"Yes ma'am," I said as I pulled up my pants. From that day on, my homeroom teacher started being very nice to me.

"Did you eat breakfast this morning, Karen?" She would ask.

"Only a boiled egg," I would reply. Helen never fed me very much in the morning, my teacher would look at me with such a sad face and then take me to the back room and feed me cereal, donuts, and orange juice. She even started bringing me clothes to school. No matter how I did in class, she would always give me a good grade.

One week after school let out for the summer, Helen got so angry with me that she twisted my arm until she broke it. She had me soaking my arm in dishwater in the kitchen sink. When my father returned home that evening, he must have realized my arm was broken because that was the first time he ever took me to the hospital after Helen had injured me. I did not return to my father's house that night, instead the doctor put a cast on my arm, and I was sent to Children Services. I spent about eight months living with foster families before I was sent back home.

CHAPTER 2

DECEMBER 1974

By the time I was nine, Helen had given birth to two children. A little girl named Candace, and a little boy named Tony Jr. Candace was the older of her two children, but she was too young to do anything to stop the abuse. Sometimes she would sit next to my door and cry. Helen never abused her own children.

Six months before Christmas, Helen started telling me that I was not going to get any presents. On Christmas day I peeked out my bedroom door and looked at the beautiful Christmas tree and all the gifts that was under it, Helen saw me peeking out the door, my father had not returned home yet.

"I don't know what you're looking at; there is nothing out here for you," she said in a very stern voice. I slowly closed the door and sat down on the bed.

On Jesus' Birthday I was released from my prison. That was the last Christmas I lived with my father and his wife. That afternoon when my dad came home from his night out, he walked into my room.

"Let me see what Santa brought you for Christmas," he said smiling. I looked at him with a frown. Surely, he knew I did not get any gifts.

"Helen said I didn't get any gifts for Christmas this year." I said with tears. I could see from the look on my fathers face that he was surprised, and then the look turned angry.

"Get your clothes on Karen. You are going to my mother's house," he said before going back into the living room.

"Okay," I said as I started putting on my clothes and shoes. Something must have told me I was not coming back, because I quickly picked up my mother and Grandma Ellis's pictures off the dresser. I could hear Helen and my dad arguing as I put my coat on.

"Come on Karen!" My dad yelled from the living room. I walked out of my bedroom toward the back door.

"Take the little tramp with you! You are turning her into a little freak! I know what you have been doing to her in the basement. I am sick of taking care of your bastard child anyway!" Helen screamed as we walked out the back door.

It had snowed the day before. I sat in the back seat in silence, staring out the window admiring all the Christmas lights and snowmen, as my father drove to my grandmother's house. I had not seen my grandmother since Grandma Ellis's funeral. All of my aunts, uncles, and cousins were at her apartment celebrating the holidays. When my father brought me into the house, everyone just stared at me.

"Bring her inside!" Aunt Grace yelled.

"What have you and Helen been doing to this girl?" My grandmother asked. I looked nothing like I looked years earlier when she had last seen me. Grandma Ellis always made sure that I looked like a little princess. Now I looked like a homeless orphan. I had on an old shirt that was so small you could see my belly button. My hair was short and nappy and I had bald spots in my head from not having my hair combed for days at a time. My shoes were torn and had holes in them.

"I just need to keep her here for a few days." My father mumbled. All my cousins walked toward me and surrounded me, staring at me as if I was a clown from a circus show. I was so skinny that I had to put safety pins in my high water pants to keep them from falling down. One of my cousins walked over to me and grabbed me by the hand.

"Hi, my name is Linda, what's your name?" She asked with a smile on her face.

"Karen," I answered shyly. I had never seen Linda before.

"Come on Karen; let me show you what my dad bought me for Christmas," she said with excitement as she motioned for me to follow her up the stairs. I liked her instantly.

A week after Christmas my father came over to my grandmother's house with a large box of toys, I had received Christmas gifts after all. It was the happiest I had felt since Grandma Ellis was alive.

The next week after I received the toys, my father came back to my grandmothers house to take me home, my aunts and uncles were there that day playing poker at the kitchen table. I overheard Aunt Grace and Uncle Jason talking to my grandmother the week before, telling her that she could not send me back with my father, it was obvious to them that they were mistreating me. Aunt Grace and Uncle Jason were my dad's younger sister and brother. They both resembled my grandmother in appearance, I really liked Uncle Jason, during the two weeks that I had been staying with my grandmother, he brought Linda over every day to play with me. He even took us out to the movies to see Superman and to Pizza Hut.

"There is no way in hell you are taking that child back to that hell hole!" My grandmother yelled putting her fist on her hips.

"That's my daughter and she is coming with me!" My father screamed back.

"Tony, I advise you to leave before someone gets hurt, Karen is going to be living with our mother she is not going back to that hell hole!" Uncle Jason yelled. Uncle Jason was a very tall and muscular man. If I had not known him, I would have thought he was a professional wrestler. My cousin Linda grabbed my hand pulling me.

"Come on Karen, let's go upstairs," she whispered as she led me out of the kitchen. Linda and I were the same age and she was Uncle Jason's only child, I always thought she was so lucky to have such a kind and loving father.

Linda and I had grown very close in the short period of time that I had been staying with my grandmother.

"Okay." I answered as I followed her. I did not want to go back and stay with my father. I could hear a lot of yelling down stairs, and the sound of fighting, and then I heard my father's car speed off. That night while lying in the bed, I took out the pictures of my mother and Grandma Ellis. Tears started flowing down my face as I kissed both pictures.

"God thank you for letting mommy and Grandma Ellis be my guardian angels. I knew the two of you would save me one day. I promise that if I ever have children, I will never let anyone treat them the way I have been treated." I whispered aloud as tears started rolling down my cheeks. I held the pictures against my chest as I lay back on the pillows.

Shortly after I moved in with my grandmother, she began asking me questions, "Karen, I want you to tell me what happened while you were living with your dad and Helen." For the first time, I felt that I could talk to someone, I felt safe. I knew that my grandmother was not going to send me back to live with my father.

"They did a lot of bad things to me."

"Like what, you don't have to be afraid to tell me."

"My dad would always take me down to the basement and touch me with his private area." I whispered. I saw the look of surprise on my grandmother's face.

"What else happened?" She asked.

I stood up and pulled down my pants, exposing my thin legs and pointed to the ugly scar on my thigh.

"Helen did this to my leg with jumper cables." My grandmother walked over to me and gently ran her hand across the scar. Then she did something that surprised me, she started crying.

"You are safe now Karen, You will never have to live with them again."

My grandmother did not waste any time going to children services and getting custody of me. When I told the children services worker about Helen, and how she made me eat her feces wrapped in bread, and how she had forced me to eat my vomit, the woman did not believe me. She sat there with a stern look on her face.

"Karen, I know that you want to live with your grandmother, but you must not make up stories," she said in a scolding voice. It frustrated me that she did not believe me. So I stopped sharing my experiences, and just said what ever I thought she wanted to hear. After a while, I really did not care if she did not believe me, I knew that it was all true.

My grandmother had me going to see a child psychologist. I had to go and see the old woman once a week. In each session, she asked me questions about the abuse. She always listened and never judged me or called me a liar. I felt comfortable talking to her. I told her things I had not even shared with my grandmother. On one visit, she had two dolls and she asked me to demonstrate what my father had done to me. When I showed her, she did not say anything, she just wrote things on a sheet of paper. I really did not understand why I had to use the dolls, I felt like I was old enough to tell her.

About six months after moving in with my grandmother, Children Services and the Franklin County Court System gave my grandmother full custody. My grandmother told me that my father and Helen never showed up for court. The police department took no legal action against them.

My grandmother was not as affectionate and loving as Grandma Ellis had been. However, she was very protective and always concerned about my well being, even if she did not always express it in words.

SPOUSE ABUSE

PART II

I sit at the table and cry, holding an ice pack to my eye,

Another horrible night, another horrible fight.

This can't be love; love does not hurt like this,

Love does not require you to use your fist.

You say I am your queen and you hate it when I make you mean.

You say that you love me and hate to see me cry.

I feel like this is all a lie.

I know God is near.

I cannot continue to live in fear.

I know that I need to leave.

The pastor said all I need to do is take a step of faith and believe.

CHAPTER 3

After a few years, my father started coming around on holidays. He never spoke of the abuse, and everyone acted like it had never happened when he was around. I did not hate my father. Linda would sometimes ask me if I wanted to do something bad to them in order to get revenge.

"God will make them pay one day." I would reply.

I went through my school years in a daze. I was very quiet and shy, I never had any true friends except for Linda. My grandmother was very strict and did not allow me to do a lot of after school activities. Linda's father was also very strict on her.

Linda and I made a pack that we would attend all the football games and parties that we could in our 12th grade year.

My grandmother never allowed me to have any boyfriends. Once when I was fourteen, a young man walked me home from the bus stop, my grandmother decided it was time to lay down the rules.

"You are not allowed to have any phone calls from boys until you are sixteen, and you cannot go out on dates until you are eighteen. You will not be bringing any babies into this house." My grandmother said frowning. I never disrespected my grandmother. She was overprotective, but I still managed to somewhat enjoy my teenage years.

Everyone at school thought I was a nerd. I usually sat somewhere in the back of the class and read romance novels while my teachers taught. I had actually grown into a very nice looking young lady. My body was in great shape and I had curves in all the right places. My grandmother use to tell me that I was a beautiful little black girl. I guess the guys just thought I was too much of a nerd, so they never asked me out on a date.

Linda was the complete opposite. All the guys liked her. Even though her father was strict, Linda had no problem with sneaking out of the house once she knew her parents were asleep. Linda looked a lot like my grandmother except for a lighter version.

Her mother was a biracial woman with long hair and hazel eyes. Linda inherited her mother's hair and eye color. Whenever we walked to the corner store together, men always whistled at her, or tried to get her telephone number.

After Linda and I graduated from high school, we enrolled in Columbus State Community College and majored in nursing. I always wanted to be a nurse. When Linda and I were young, we would play as if we were at the hospital. I was always the nurse and she was the patient. I guess I just wanted to take care of people who were sick or wounded. I had a special love for infants; my dream was to become an obstetrics nurse or a neonatal nurse, or both if I could.

I had a part time job working at the Columbus Police Department as a clerk. This is where I met Clyde King. Clyde was a police officer and very popular with the women. All the women at work talked about him constantly. I would listen to them during breaks, all of them wishing he would ask them out on a date. Some of the women were even bold enough to flirt with him openly. Whenever he would walk by, they would drool as if he were Elvis. Clyde was about six feet tall, and about 250 pounds of hard, lean muscles. You could see his bulging muscles when he had on his uniforms. He had naturally curly hair and light hazel eyes. He was the color of caramel candy and had the sexiest smile I had ever seen on a man. The day Clyde asked me out to dinner I was completely surprised. I was sitting at the front desk when he came up to me from out of nowhere.

"Hello Miss. White," he said. I had my head down doing paper work so I did not even see him walk up to the desk.

"Hello Clyde," I said with a big smile. He was so sexy. He was leaning on my desk as if he was the head of the department.

"What are you doing after work today?"

"I don't have any plans." I replied as I glanced at my coworker who was sitting next to me, staring at us.

"Can I take you out to dinner?" He asked.

"Sure," I replied. I could not believe that this man was actually asking me out on a date.

"Cool, I have to work second shift tonight, but I will have about an hour for dinner. What time do you get off?" He asked as he glanced at his watch.

"I get off at 4:30." I could feel my palms starting to sweat. Whenever I became nervous or anxious about something, my hands would always sweat.

"Okay, it's a date. I will be back at 4:30." He gave me a big smile. As soon as he walked away my coworker, Angel started in on me.

"Wow, did I just hear him ask you out on a date?" She asked with a surprised look on her face.

"Yes, I guess he did." I answered as I finished shuffling through the paperwork on my desk. Angel and I had been working beside each other for the last three months. We never spoke to each other unless it was pertaining to our job.

"Girl, every woman in here has been dying to go out with him," she said still staring at me with her mouth hanging open and an amazed look on her face. I did not respond I really did not want my business all over the police department. Even though Angel and I did not talk much, I knew that she was a gossip column. I had heard her spreading someone else's business around the office more than once. At 4:30 p.m. on the dot, Clyde was standing at the front desk waiting for me to clock out.

"Where would you like to go?" He asked as I walked from behind the desk.

"Oh, I don't know anywhere you would like to take me." When we reached his Ford Explorer, he opened the door for me like a true gentleman. He decided to take me to Applebee's.

"Order anything that you would like," he said as we sat down in a booth near the window. When the server finally came over to our table, I ordered ribs, baked potato, cheese noodles, and lemonade. Clyde ordered steak, baked potato, broccoli, and a double rum and coke on the rocks.

"Aren't you still on duty?" I asked, after the server walked away.

"Yea, but a little drink won't harm anything. It relaxes me. It's hard work chasing after criminals all day," he replied.

"How many years have you been a police officer?" I asked shyly.

"I joined the force about fifteen years ago, right after I was discharged from the Army." The server walked up to our table and set our drinks down on napkins.

"Is there anything else I can get for you sir?" She did not even look at me. She was to busy staring at Clyde.

"No that will be all for now," he said smiling. She glanced at me with a smirk and walked away from the table. She was switching her butt so hard; it would have flown out the window if it were not for her spine. I saw Clyde watching her walk away before he returned his attention to me. I felt a little tinge of jealousy.

"So, tell me Miss. White, where is your boyfriend?" He asked as he took a sip of his drink.

"I don't have one," I answered as I took a sip from my glass of lemonade.

"What, a beautiful chocolate woman like you does not have a man protecting her. This must be my lucky day," he said winking at me. I felt myself blush.

"How old are you Miss. White, if you don't mind me asking?"

"Nineteen." I answered as I took another sip of my lemonade.

"How old are you, Clyde?" I knew he was a lot older than I was.

"Thirty-eight, is that too old for you?" He asked as he reached across the table and held my hand.

"No, thirty-eight is not that old. It just means you are very mature." I replied as I gently pulled my hand away and put my hands in my lap. I could feel my palms starting to sweat. He did not say anything. He just looked at me. Somehow I felt like his beautiful hazel eyes were reading my soul.

"What made you want to ask me out for dinner? All the women at work drool over you, you could have any of them, why me?"

"Well, I have been watching you for the last few months. I think you are the most beautiful dark skin woman I have ever seen, you are very sexy, and you always carry yourself like a lady. Most of the women at work have already slept with half of the men on the force, I am not interested in dating tramps." The server returned before I had a chance to reply, she placed our food on the table.

"Would you like anything else?" She asked giving Clyde a huge smile. I was really starting to get irritated with this server, she was completely ignoring me.

"No, that will be all for now." We continued to talk over dinner. He asked all the questions and I answered.

When we were ready to leave, I gave him directions on how to get to my apartment. It was a relief to get a ride home, since I always had to take the long ride home on the Cota bus. We pulled up in front of my grandmother's apartment complex. He got out of the truck and escorted me to my front door. I glanced at the window and saw my grandmother peeking through the blinds.

"Thank you for dinner. I enjoyed myself." I said as I searched in my purse for my keys.

"Can we do this again tomorrow?" He asked.

"Yes, I would like that."

"Cool. I will see you tomorrow." He turned and walked back down the steps.

"So who was that?" My grandmother asked as soon as I walked into the apartment.

"He is a police officer; he works at the department with me." I answered as I walked toward the kitchen and put my keys and purse on the table. She followed me into the kitchen.

"I can't tell you what to do anymore, but if you wind up pregnant, I am kicking your butt out of the house, I am not taking care of any more children," she said with narrowed eyes.

"Grandmother, he just gave me a ride home." I walked up to my room and closed the door. I always went straight to my room when I got home. My bedroom was a sacred place to me. I guess it came from years of Helen locking me in my room.

Sometimes my grandmother would get frustrated, she felt like I spent too much time there.

"Karen, get out of that room and come clean up the kitchen. You act like that room is your apartment!" She would yell.

I had to call Linda and let her know about my day. I sat down on my bed and picked up the telephone, dialing her phone number.

"Hello," she answered.

"What's up Linda, you will never guess what happened to me today. I had my first real date."

"What?" She screamed into the phone in an excited voice.

"I am on my way over. I have got to hear about this in person," she stated before hanging up the phone. Linda still lived at home with Uncle Jason and Aunt Susie, her parents only lived fifteen minutes away. Uncle Jason took good care of Linda.

Unlike me, she did not have to work because her dad still gave her allowance money, her dad was a prosecutor for the State of Ohio. Linda was the only woman I knew whose parents still spoiled her. There was a knock on my bedroom door; I already knew who it was before I answered the door.

"Come in Linda," I said excitedly. I was anxious to tell her about my date.

She opened the door and immediately came into my room and sat down on my bed.

"Okay, tell me everything, and you better not leave out one single detail"

I told her about how he approached me. What my coworker had said, how the women drooled over him at work, our dinner date, and how our grandmother had acted when I got home.

"Don't let grandmother get you upset. You know she loves you, she does not always know how to show it. She just wants to protect you."

"Yea, but sometimes she goes overboard." I said with a frown on my face.

"So is he really that cute?" She asked as she flipped through my latest edition of Essence Magazine.

"Cute is not the word. This brother is fine. I still can't believe he is interested in me." I sighed.

"Are the two of you going out again?"

"Yes, he asked me out for dinner again tomorrow." I said as I stood up and walked over to my dresser and glanced in the mirror.

"How old is he?"

"Thirty-eight."

"Wow. He is an older man. I dated an older man once. He use to spoil me and give me money all the time. I stopped dating him when his wife found out about us."

She said still glancing through the magazine. Linda usually told me everything, for some reason I did not remember her talking about dating an older married man.

"When did this happen?" I asked walking back over to the bed and sitting down beside her.

"When I was in the 11th grade, I didn't tell anyone because I didn't want anyone to know. If my dad had even guessed that I was messing around with someone that old, he would have had him up on charges so fast it would have made the guys head spin," she laughed. I did not laugh. I was hurt that Linda did not trust me enough to confide in me.

"I would not have said anything." I said slightly raising my voice.

"I know but he made me promise I would not tell anyone."

"Did you sleep with him?" I asked. I knew that my cousin was no virgin. She looked at me and smiled.

"Yes, and let me tell you, older men know how to make love much better than younger men do, I guess it's because they are more experienced."

I had never had sex with a man before. I still considered my self a virgin, even though my father molested me as a child. I knew he had never been able to penetrate me and that my hymen was still intact.

"Do you think you can handle an older man?" She asked.

"I don't know, but I guess I will find out" I said winking at her.

"You go girl." Linda said hitting me gently on my thigh with the magazine she was holding in her hand.

22

"I have tried to hook you up so many times, but you would never give them a chance. I am glad you decided to loosen up" Linda said jokingly.

"That's because all the men you tried to hook me up with always looked like a nerd." We both started laughing.

She stayed over my house for another thirty-five minutes, telling me about her newest boyfriend, and the car that her dad said he was going to buy her for her 20th birthday. Then she rushed home so that she could get ready for our evening classes at Columbus State.

CHAPTER 4

Over the next four months, Clyde started taking me out to dinner almost every night after work. After a while, he even started picking me up from Columbus State after my evening classes and giving me a ride home. He never tried to kiss me or even get sexual with me. He was always the perfect gentleman. I was glad because I had never kissed anyone before. When he first started bringing me home, my grandmother would always have something negative to say. After a while, Clyde won her over and she started greeting him at the door.

One night when he came to pick me up from school, he told me that he was not taking me straight home. He said he had a surprise for me.

"What is it?" I asked with anticipation.

"You will see," he said as he drove on the exit ramp to 71 north. I was starting to feel comfortable around Clyde, everyone at work knew Clyde and I were dating. It felt good for the women to know I had such a handsome man interested in me.

Sometimes I would get nasty looks from the ones who were jealous.

I noticed that we had gotten off on the Morse road exit, I knew we were headed toward his house. We had stopped at his house a few other times on our way home from work. I always declined when he asked me if I wanted to go inside.

"Why are we stopping at your house?" I asked.

"The surprise that I have for you is in my house, come on inside," he stated as he got out of the truck. He did not wait for me to follow; he started walking toward his front door. I got out of the truck and followed him inside his house. Clyde had a nicely decorated house, it was not glamorous or anything, it just felt nice and cozy. I followed him into his family room and was surprised when I saw all the beautiful flowers, and the balloons with the words, "Will You Marry Me," floating all over the room. He came over to me, grabbed my hand, and got down on one knee.

"Will you give me the honor of marrying me and being my wife?" He asked.

I was completely surprised. This was not what I had expected.

"Clyde, we have only been seeing each other for four months." I said as he held my hand.

"I love you Karen, I want you to be my wife. I do not need to be with someone for ten years to know if they are the one for me. I am not getting any younger, I want children. I told you that my first wife and I never had any children together before she died. I am ready to settle down and have a family. I cannot think of anyone else I would want to be my wife and bare my children. You are my heart and I have fallen deeply in love with you," he said as he kissed my hand. Tears were developing in my eyes. No one had ever said anything like that to me before. I did feel like I cared deeply for him. He reached into his pocket and pulled out a little black box and handed it to me. I opened it and smiled at the diamond engagement ring.

"I want to spend the rest of my life with you; will you have me as your husband?"

"Yes Clyde, I will marry you."

"You are going to make me the happiest man on earth," he said as he took the ring out of the box and placed it on my left ring finger. That night we kissed for the very first time, I felt so stupid and immature. I did not know what to do when he slid his tongue into my mouth.

"Don't worry baby, I will teach you every thing you need to know about kissing and how to please me in the bedroom, after we are married." He chuckled, then he grabbed my hand and led me out of the house and back into his truck. As soon as I got home, I called Linda.

"Linda, Clyde asked me to marry him today!" I yelled into the phone as I jumped up and down on my bed. I was so happy; I just kept staring at the beautiful ring on my finger.

"He asked you to marry him?" I could hear the surprise in her voice, "You two have only been dating for a few months, and you have never even been inside his house."

"I went in tonight, he had balloons and flowers all over the house, he even gave me an engagement ring," I said as I sat down on the bed.

"So what was your answer?"

"I said yes," I replied polishing the small diamond with the corner of my sheet.

"Karen, you don't even know him that well." I was starting to get a little irritated with her attitude. I thought she would be happy for me. Instead she was interrogating me.

"I know that I love him, that's all that really matters, anyway lots of people get married right after they meet. I see talk shows about it all the time." I said in a defensive voice.

"Well, if you are sure Karen. I just want you to be happy," she said with a sigh.

"I will be." I replied. Linda always felt like she had to protect me. We talked a little longer about the homework assignment that was due the next day, and then we hung up the phone. I pulled out the pictures of my mom and Grandma Ellis.

"Guess what mommy and Grandma Ellis, I am about to get married to a handsome police officer, I know he will take good care of me." I said aloud. I smiled at the pictures and then put them away. That night I lay in my bed awake half the night, fantasizing about my new life with Clyde King and all the beautiful children we would have together.

Clyde and I were married three months later at the courthouse. He said he did not want to waste a lot of money on a big wedding. I was a little disappointed, I always imagined that when I got married I would be wearing a beautiful white gown, and walking down the aisle of a large church. I guess as long as I was marrying someone I loved, it really did not matter where we said our vows. My grandmother and Linda were at the courthouse with us. My family planned a small reception at Uncle Jason's house. No one from Clyde's family attended the wedding or the reception.

We went to Kings Island for our honeymoon. Clyde paid for a nice suite at one of the hotels near Kings Island. We had a lot of fun, riding rides and playing games. That night we went out to a club in down town Cincinnati, Ohio. I was so nervous, I knew that once we left the club, it would be time to go back to the hotel and consummate our wedding vows. I had heard many stories about how painful a woman's first sexual experience can be. Linda told me that I would probably bleed a lot the first time.

Clyde was really enjoying himself. I noticed for the first time that he really liked to drink a lot of alcohol. He had at least two double rum and cokes and three beers before we left the club. I was concerned about him getting us back to the hotel room safely.

"I am just fine. Do not worry honey. I can hold my liqueur," he said as we got into his truck. He was clearly intoxicated when we got back to the room, but he still insisted on ordering another drink from room service.

"Go get ready for bed Karen," he said while on the telephone.

"Okay." I answered. I picked up my traveling case off the edge of the bed and walked into the bathroom. I took a long hot shower, massaged my body with scented lotion, and then put on the negligee Linda bought me for a wedding gift.

By the time I came out of the bathroom, room service had brought him another drink. He kissed me on the cheek as I sat down on the king size bed, and then he walked into the bathroom and closed the door.

The room Clyde selected was nice. It had an adjoining room, a kitchenette, and a small sitting room. I was trying to concentrate on not being nervous when he finally got out of the shower. He sat down on a chair across from our bed and motioned for me to come to him. He was naked, which right away made me feel uncomfortable. I had never seen a man completely naked. I walked over to where he was sitting and stood in front of him.

"Kneel right here," he said pointing toward the floor. I did as he asked. He put his hand behind my head, picked up his manhood with his other hand, and started pushing my head toward it.

"What are you doing Clyde?" I asked as I yanked my head away and stood up.

"Karen, we are married now, there is no need to be shy." He said slurring his words.

"That's something I will not do." I said with wide eyes. I could not believe he really thought I was going to do something like that. He stood up staggering slightly and looked at me.

"The first thing you need to learn is what I expect and how to please me."

"Well that's not one of the things I am willing to learn. I think it's nasty." I said wrinkling up my face to show him my disgust. I walked over to the bed and sat down. There was no way I was going to put my mouth on him. In my high school, girls who performed oral sex were whores and sluts.

He stared at me for a long time. His soft, sexy looks suddenly changed; taking its place was a hard cold expression. He walked over to me and before I could react, he slapped me in the face. I grabbed my cheek and looked up at him in complete shock.

"You are my wife; you will do what I tell you to do, when I tell you to do it." Then he pushed me back on the bed and jumped on top of me. I started wrestling with him trying to push him off me. "Clyde get off of me you are drunk!" I said breathlessly. It seemed like he did not hear me. He tried to kiss me in the mouth, but I turned my head to the side. The smell of liqueur on his breath made me nauseous. He pushed my legs apart with his knee as he held both of my arms above my head. I was no match for him. His strength over powered me. I felt his hard shaft enter me roughly. Then I felt a horrible pain as he thrust his manhood inside of me. I let out a loud scream. The pain was almost unbearable. He put his hand over my mouth, silencing my screams. He continued to thrust in and out of me with quick hard force. His thrust picked up speed, and then just as suddenly as he started, he let out a loud moan, and fell on top of me. I started crying. I never imagined that my husband would rape me on my honeymoon. He rolled off me and passed out. I stood up and went to the bathroom. I picked up a washcloth off the sink, wet it, and then wiped in between my thighs. I saw a lot of blood on my washcloth. I cleaned myself up, then went back to the bed and laid down on my side facing away from him and started crying. I was asleep when a sharp pain awakened me. I was lying flat on my stomach. Clyde was lying on my back. I could feel his manhood inside my buttocks. The pain that I felt was even worse than the pain from earlier that evening.

"Clyde, Stop it!" I screamed, trying to buck and throw him off my back.

His weight pinned me down and I could not move. I screamed as he thrust his manhood further and further into my buttocks.

"Someone please help me!" I screamed.

29

He put his hand over my mouth and continued thrusting faster and faster until he climaxed, then he stopped and leaned close to my ear, "You are my wife Karen. Your body is no longer yours, its mine. You will learn to please me and you will do what I ask you to do or I will make you do it." Clyde whispered, and then he rolled off me and walked to the bathroom.

After two days of being raped by my husband, I finally gave in and performed oral sex on him, I felt more like a slut than a new bride. I felt humiliated and degraded.

What happened to the kind man I fell in love with and thought I married? After I performed oral sex on him, he was nice to me again, as if nothing bad had ever happened.

When we returned home, I went straight upstairs to the spare bedroom. I did not want to be in the same bedroom with Clyde. He followed me up the stairs.

"No, Karen, this is not where you will be sleeping. We are husband and wife.

We will be sharing the same room," he said as he grabbed the suitcase out of my hand. I looked at him in disgust and walked toward our bedroom.

"You need to get use to satisfying your husband, consider yourself in training," he said as he closed our bedroom door and began unbuttoning his pants.

I was sore from the front to the back. I winced in pain every time I went to the bathroom.

"Clyde, I'm sore. I don't feel like having sex." I said as I sat down on the bed. He walked over to the bed and grabbed my chin, forcing my head up.

"It's no longer about what you want it is about pleasing me," Clyde said in a low voice. I did not have any more fight in me. I knew he would get angry and hit me as he had done in the hotel room if I tried to resist. After we had sex, he went into the bathroom and took a shower. I sat on the bed with tears in my eyes. He had made it clear that I was now his property. As his wife, I had to perform whatever sexual acts he wanted, when he wanted.

After he finished taking his shower, he walked back into the bedroom and began putting on his police uniform.

"I have to work tonight. Tomorrow we will go down town and start changing all of your identification cards to Karen King."

After He left, I glanced at the clock. It was time to get ready for class. I knew Linda would be waiting to ask me the details of our honeymoon. I didn't want her or anyone else to know what my new husband had made me do. I thought about skipping class, but with finals only a few weeks away, I decided that would not be a good idea. So I started getting ready.

When I arrived on campus, I went straight to my anatomy class. Linda was already there. When she saw me come into the room, she motioned for me to sit in the seat next to her.

"So Mrs. King how was your honeymoon?" She asked with a big smile as I sat down.

"It was fine." I replied shrugging my shoulders as I began opening my notebook and glancing over the notes, I had written from our last lecture.

"That's it, just fine?" She shrugged her shoulders imitating my gesture.

"Kings Island was a lot of fun," I said casually. The professor walked into the classroom and began addressing the class before Linda had a chance to ask me any more questions. I was relieved. If she had kept pressing me, I would have started crying again.

After my last class, I caught the Cota bus over to my grandmother's house. I wanted to get some more of my things, and I was not ready to go back home. My grandmother was not at home when I got there. "She must be at bingo." I said aloud.

I went up to my bedroom and started packing my things. I wanted to make sure that I did not forget my mother, and Grandma Ellis's pictures. I made a mental note to remind myself to get new frames for their pictures. I grabbed what I could carry and went out to catch the bus.

When I finally made it back home, I saw Clyde's police car in the driveway. It's funny, as a new wife, I should have been excited to see my husband, but instead I felt apprehensive. I unlocked the door to find him pacing up and down the hallway with a telephone in his hand, when he saw me come through the door he stopped walking and just stared at me.

"Ms White, she just walked in the door," he said into the telephone.

"Here, your grandmother wants to speak to you," he said as he handed me the phone with a mean look on his face. I took the phone from him and walked into the living room. "Hi Grandmother, I just left your house." I said nonchalantly.

She immediately started fussing at me about getting Clyde upset. She told me I needed to make sure that I checked in with my husband when I was going to go somewhere so that he would not worry about me. I explained to her that I had gone to class. After a few more minutes of listening to her fuss, I assured her that everything was okay, and then we hung up.

"Karen, you will not be returning to Columbus State, you don't need it. I do not want all those men around my wife. I never felt comfortable with you going there anyway, that is why I started picking you up from school every night. I also want you to put in your resignation. You will not need to work anymore. I will take care of all the bills. Your job will be to maintain our home, keep it clean, and cook our meals." He said as he sat down on the couch. I could not believe what I was hearing.

"I am not quitting school or my job. You are taking this marriage thing too far! You do not own me Clyde!" I yelled as I ran up the steps to our bedroom.

I could hear him running up the steps after me. Before I could get the door closed to lock it, he pushed it open with so much force; I almost fell on the floor. He grabbed me and pushed me up against the wall by my neck. He was squeezing my neck so hard I could hardly breathe. He put his face close to mine. I could smell alcohol on his breath. He gave me a cold stare that sent chills down my spine.

"I am not going to keep telling you that you will obey me," he said as he tightened his grip around my neck. I was starting to feel light headed. My eyes were wide with fear.

"If you ever talk back to me like that again, I will break your neck." Just as quickly as he had grabbed me, he released me and pushed me onto the bed.

"Clyde, you don't own me!" I screamed defiantly. Tears were streaming down my face. He looked at me long and hard, then he pulled his belt out of his pants and started hitting me with it. I screamed in pain and tried to run but he grabbed me by my ponytail and put me in a headlock. He sat down on the bed so that my buttocks would be up in the air. He yanked my skirt up, pulled down my panties, and started hitting me on the butt and back with his belt.

"You will obey me Karen!" He yelled. I screamed and screamed until I felt like my head would explode from the pressure and pain I was enduring. He beat me for what seemed like an eternity. Then he released me, pushing me onto the floor. He pulled his pants off and jumped on top of me, spreading my legs with his thigh, I bite him on his arm. He yelled out in pain and smacked me in the face with his hand. I suddenly felt dizzy; all the fight was gone out of me as he thrust his hard manhood inside of me.

"You are mine," he whispered in my ear. After he climaxed, he stood up and sat on the bed. Then he got dressed and left the room. A few minutes later, I heard his car leave the driveway. I got up off the floor and walked into the bathroom. I went to the mirror and looked at my swollen lip, then I turned to the side so that I could see what damage had been done to my backside. There were whelps from his belt all over my back and butt. Now I knew how slaves must have felt after their masters beat them. I sat down on the toilet and started crying. I was going through torture all over again. The only difference was that instead of it being my father and stepmother torturing me, now it was my husband.

CHAPTER 5

The next morning Clyde took me down town to change my name on my driver's license and social security card. Then he took me to withdraw from Columbus State. I called my supervisor at the police department and told him that I would not be returning. After we were finished, he took me to lunch and then dropped me off at home.

"Make sure that dinner is cooked when I get home and I want you to iron all my uniforms and hang them up in the closet." Then he pulled off. There was no way I was going to stay with this monster. I walked to the bus stop and caught the Cota bus to my grandmother's house. When I got there, she was sitting on the sofa watching, 'The Guiding Light.' I guess she could see from the expression on my face that something was wrong.

"Is something bothering you Karen?" She asked.

"I want to come back home and live with you; I do not want to stay married to Clyde."

"Why not, he is your husband?" She asked frowning at me.

"He is not the man I thought he was. He beat me last night." I said glancing at the floor. I did not want her to see the sadness in my eyes. She stood up and walked over to where I was standing and gave me a stern look. I could feel a sermon coming.

"I told you from the beginning to leave that man alone, but you would not listen. Well it is too late now, he is your husband and you have to stay with him. You cannot come back and stay here." My shoulders dropped in disappointment.

"I raised you the best that I could. You're grown now, and a wife's place is with her husband," she said, putting her hands on her hips. "Things will not always be easy, but you have to try and make it work.

35

I was married to your grandfather for thirty years before he passed away, there were many times I wanted to leave him because I thought he was not treating me right, but I didn't because we made vows before God and I took those vows seriously. You have only been married to Clyde for a few days and already you are trying to run. You had better grow up Karen; you're not a child anymore." She said and then walked to the kitchen.

That night I cooked baked chicken, broccoli, mash potatoes, and rolls for dinner.

I also did as he had instructed and ironed all of his work clothes and hung them in the closet. I guess my grandmother was right. I had decided to marry Clyde, so now I had to stay with him, I made vows before God. When he got home that night dinner was waiting on him. "Something smells good," he said as he walked in the door and hung up his coat. I did not respond, I continued to watch TV. He walked over to the couch and sat down next to me.

"Karen, I love you, I don't like hurting you. You are my queen, the future mother of my unborn children. I want us to be happy together," he said as he put his hand on my knee. I started crying. It seemed like all I had done over the last few days was cry.

"If you love me, then why are you treating me this way?" I asked in between sobs.

He pulled some tissue out of the decorated tissue box on the living room table and handed it to me. I took the tissue from him, wiped my eyes and blew my nose.

"I hate to see you cry. I love you baby. I just want you to understand that I am now your husband and you must act like my wife. I know you are only nineteen and inexperienced but you will learn." He got up and walked to the kitchen. Just as he was walking away, the telephone rang.

"Hello?" I answered. The phone went dead. "I guess it was a wrong number." I said to myself as I replaced the phone on the receiver. Twenty minutes later the telephone rang again. This time Clyde answered the phone.

"Karen, Linda is on the phone." Clyde yelled from the kitchen. I picked up the cordless phone that was on the table next to me.

"Hello?" I answered as I started walking upstairs to my bedroom. I did not want Clyde to listen to my conversation.

"What's up girl, I missed you in class today? You know that we have finals coming up in two weeks. This is not the time to start missing class. That section on the nervous system is hard." I knew Linda would call me when she saw that I was not in class, I had never missed class in the whole year that we had been in school.

"I won't be coming back to class Linda." I said in a low voice.

"What!" Linda shouted in the phone. "I know you are not trying to tell me that you dropped out?"

"Yes I did."

"Why in the hell would you drop out of class? We are almost at the end of the quarter. We only have two weeks left until finals and you were carrying a 95% in all your classes."

"Clyde felt I needed to be at home since we are newly married." I said in a low voice.

"Doesn't he know that all you have ever wanted to do was get your R.N. and become an obstetrics nurse so that you could take care of babies and pregnant women?"

She asked. I was starting to get frustrated. Linda just did not understand.

"Linda, I have to go, I will call you back later." I hung up the phone before she had a chance to reply. The last thing I wanted to talk about was school. When Linda and I were young, all we ever talked about was becoming nurses so that we could save the world. We had made plans to go to school together, work at the same hospital, marry doctors, and live in mansions right next door to each other. I guess our childhood dreams were not going to come true.

Over the next twelve months, I tried to do what my grandmother said. I tried to be a good wife. Sometimes it seemed like my husband had two personalities. Half of the time, he would be very loving and kind toward me. He would take me out to dinner, movies, bring me home gifts and flowers, but other times he was very cruel, especially when he had been drinking. Clyde would come home and start beating on me for something small, like not cleaning up the kitchen or forgetting to take a telephone message for him.

The worst beating I received from him was after I experienced a miscarriage, I had been pregnant for two months when I started bleeding heavy and having severe cramps. I called Linda and she drove me to the hospital.

When Clyde found out, he beat me so bad I thought he was going to kill me. He told me that it was my fault and I had killed his baby on purpose. I spent a week in the hospital after that beating, I never called the police. I did not want to have my husband put behind bars, I also did not want the police department to find out that Clyde was beating his wife. I lied and told everyone including my family, that I had been mugged and didn't see who my perpetrator was. After the beatings, Clyde was always apologetic, begging for forgiveness.

I had also grown accustomed to his sexual demands. I knew what was expected of me and I did it. He would walk into the house, take off his gun hoister, pull down his pants, and motion for me to come to him. Without a question, I would get on my knees and perform oral sex until he climaxed. If I complained about doing it too long, I would be popped in the head. After receiving a few beatings with his belt, I also learned to make sure that all meals were prepared and the house was clean by the time he got home. I was so unhappy, never knowing when my next beating was going to occur. I never knew if Clyde was going to be drunk or sober when he got home.

One evening he came home in a very good mood. I was fixing his plate when he walked into the kitchen.

"There is going to be a police ball next weekend at the Embassy Suites Hotel. Police officers from all over Ohio are going to be there. You and I are going, so I want you to go out next week and find a nice ball gown to wear. You can also get your hair and nails done," he walked over to me and handed me his credit card.

"I have to pull a double shift tonight so I will not have time to eat dinner," he said as he kissed me on the forehead. "I won't be back until sometime tomorrow afternoon."

"You have been doing a lot of double shifts lately." I said with a frown on my face. The least he could have done was call me from work and let me know that I did not have to make dinner. Of course, I would never say that to him, a statement like that would surely earn me a fat lip.

"Someone has to take care of all the bills around here." Clyde said as he picked up his jacket and left. I looked at the Visa card he had given me. "I guess there are some benefits to being married." I said aloud. I was glad that he had not tried to have sex with me before he left. I knew that tonight I would sleep in peace.

I had many things to do the week of the ball. I took Linda with me so she could help me pick out a dress. She and I did not hang out as much as we use to.

Every time we did hang out, she would take the opportunity to tell me that I needed to leave Clyde. We went to the Lazarus Department Store to try to find my dress.

Clyde told me to spend as much as I needed on my dress and shoes. We were riding the escalator, when a man behind us spoke.

"Hello ladies." Linda and I turned around to see who was talking to us.

"Hello." Linda said in one of her sexy voices.

"Hi." I said with a smile. He was a very handsome and well-built man. He looked like he was about 6 ft tall and around thirty-five year's old.

"Nice day today isn't it?" He asked as he smiled at me.

"Yes it is nice." I replied.

When we got off the escalator, Linda and I walked toward the gowns section. Linda immediately started in on me.

"You really need to leave him Karen. Just because he is your husband, does not give him the right to hit on you. I know Grandmother told you that a woman's place is with her husband, but times have changed since she was with our grandfather. Women do not have to take that kind of abuse any more."

"Linda, I do not want to talk about my marriage right now. I want to enjoy myself. If you are going to start lecturing me, you are going to mess up my day." I said with a frown. I was not in the mood for her speech today.

"Well, have you at least asked him if you can start going back to school?" She sighed.

"No, I will though." I said as I flipped through gowns on the rack. She pulled a long beautiful, white, shinny, strapless gown off the hanger and checked to see the size.

"Hey this one is nice looking; go try it on while I continue looking." I took the gown from her and walked over to the sales woman to ask for the changing room. I was relieved to get away from Linda. I did not want to talk about my life with her. I tried on a few more dresses until

I found one I really liked. It was a red strapless gown with a long split on the side. "Do you think this would be too revealing?" I asked as I stared in the mirror. The dress was beautiful. I had never been to a ball before and I was not sure how everyone would be dressed.

"I think you will look stunning." Linda said with a huge smile on her face.

After purchasing the dress, we left Lazarus and went from store to store until we found shoes to match. After we finished shopping for accessories, we found a nice Café and had lunch. I listened to her talk about the new car that her father had bought for her birthday and how well it drove, school, her new job, and the new guy she was dating.

It was late when I finally made it back home. Clyde had not gotten home yet so I started dinner. While I was in the kitchen, the telephone rang. I ran to answer it before it stopped ringing. I had flour all over my hands.

"Hello?" I said breathlessly. The phone went dead. Over the last few months I had been getting a lot of hang ups. When I told Clyde about it he had shrugged stating they were probably just people with the wrong telephone number.

Clyde returned home late that night as usual, I was already in bed when he opened the bedroom door. He took off his clothes and got in the shower. When he had finished taking his shower, he got into the bed and started pulling off my panties. I lay very quiet as he got on top of me. Most of the time he didn't even try to kiss or caress me, he would just jump on top of me, have intercourse, and then go to sleep without saying one word. I had grown to hate sex. I was guaranteed to get raped after a beating, the rapes were always brutal. There were many times I wondered if he really loved me. We didn't talk much at all except about household matters or small talk, the few times that we did have long conversations, it was usually about us having a child. He seemed obsessed with getting me pregnant and having children.

There were two things I could always count on, Clyde beating me when he was upset with me or drunk, and having sex. I felt miserable, lonely, and trapped.

CHAPTER 6

I spent all day at the full service beauty salon. Tonight was the big police ball. Clyde told me he had to work and would get dressed in his tuxedo at the police station. He said he would be home by 7:30pm and to make sure I was dressed.

I felt proud of myself; I almost did not recognize myself in the mirror. My hair stylist put burgundy streaks in my hair and put my long hair into spiral curls. She also made up my face; giving me tips on what makeup would look best on my hershey colored skin. The dress that I had chosen seemed to accent my skin color. I felt beautiful. I could see my mother's features when I looked in the mirror. I had her slanted eyes and bright smile; I knew Grandma Ellis would have been so proud if she could see me.

I heard Clyde come through the door at exactly 7:30pm.

"Come on Karen, we have to get going, I don't want to be late!" He yelled from the living room. When I walked down the stairs, he just stopped and stared. My husband was a very handsome man. Looking at him dressed in his tuxedo made me smile. I thought about the first time he asked me out to dinner. He had hypnotized me with those hazel eyes and that sexy smile. No wonder so many women at the police station had been so fascinated with him.

"You look breathtaking in that gown Mrs. King; I can't wait until I get you home tonight," Clyde said as he grabbed my hand and guided me down the last two steps. I blushed but did not say anything.

The parking lot was packed. It took us twenty minutes to find a parking space. Once we finally got inside the hotel Clyde took my hand and led me to a row of chairs near the front entrance.

"Sit in this chair baby; I will be right back with our drinks," he said smiling at me. Then he walked away. There were so many people there. Everyone was dressed in formal wear. Some of the dresses that the women had on were very revealing, I felt more relaxed with the long split in my ball gown. Clyde had been gone for about fifteen minutes when I heard a familiar voice.

"So we meet again." When I turned to see who had spoken to me I instantly recognized the man that Linda and I had met on the escalator at Lazarus.

"Must be destiny?" He said as he sat down in the chair beside me.

"Hello," I said with a smile. He was looking very handsome in his black tuxedo.

"Let me formally introduce my self. My name is John, what is your name?" He asked as he stretched out his hand for me to shake.

"Karen King." I replied as I shook his hand. He saw my wedding band and promptly released my hand. I quickly put my hand back into my lap and took a quick glance around the room. Clyde had been gone for a while. I know it did not take that long to order drinks.

"So are you here with your husband?" John asked. Just as I was about to answer,

Clyde walked up to me holding two drinks in his hand. He gave John a mean look.

"Uh, did I take your seat?" John asked looking very uncomfortable.

"Yes, actually you did, how do you know my wife?" Clyde asked without breaking a smile. John stood up so that Clyde could have his seat. Clyde did not sit down; instead, he looked John directly in the face.

"Oh we met last week. I was just saying hello. You have a beautiful wife. You are a very lucky man," he turned toward me. "It was very nice meeting you again, Karen. I hope that you enjoy your night." Then he walked away. Clyde did not say anything to me he just gave me a cold stare, handed me my drink, and sat down in a chair next to me.

I saw women that I knew from work. A few of the women even came over to us to say hello. One of the women asked Clyde for a dance. I remembered her; she was one of the women who had always talked about how fine Clyde was.

"Do you mind if I borrow your husband for a minute? He promised me a dance if I saw him here tonight," she asked with a big fake smile on her face.

"No, I don't mind." I shrugged.

"I will be right back, don't go anywhere." Clyde said getting up to follow her onto the dance floor, it seemed like as soon as Clyde walked away John came up to me; it was as if he had been waiting on the opportunity. He sat down in the chair that Clyde had occupied.

"I hope I didn't cause any problems." John said with a smile.

"No, everything is fine." I replied.

"I see that your husband is dancing. Would you like to dance? This is my favorite song?" I know that I probably should have said no, but when I glanced at the floor and seen how close my husband was dancing with his coworker, I decided to take him up on his offer.

"Yes, I would like to dance." I stood up and followed him to the dance floor. The song was an upbeat melody from the 70s. For some reason it seemed like John was purposely dancing very close to me.

"I hope that when I finally get married, it will be to a woman as beautiful as you," he said in a low sexy voice. I smiled; it felt good to receive a compliment from such a handsome man, when the song ended, I thanked him for the dance. I was surprised when he took my hand and kissed it.

"The pleasure was all mines. Tell your husband to make sure he treats you right," he said with a wink and then walked away. I went back to my chair and sat down. A few seconds later, Clyde walked up to me with a very evil look on his face.

"Let's go!" He said, grabbing my arm and pulling me out of the chair.

"What's wrong Clyde? The ball is not over yet." I asked with a worried look on my face. I had seen that look so many times before; I knew he was angry about something. Usually when I saw that look on his face he was angry with me. He led me out of the hotel and toward our Ford Explorer, once we got into the truck Clyde backhanded me in the face. It took me completely off guard; I put my hand to my nose and saw blood.

"You better not ever disrespect me like that again!" He yelled as he started the engine and pulled out of the parking lot. I started crying. I already knew what was going to happen once we got home. When we got to our house, he pulled me out of the truck and pushed me into the house. Before I could react, he started hitting me in the face, I tried to block the blows with my hands, but he was too quick for me.

"I'm sorry Clyde!" I screamed. I tried to run into the other room, but he grabbed me before I could escape and started dragging me up the steps. He grabbed his belt that he kept hanging on the closet door and started beating me with it.

"Don't you ever let another man touch you!" He yelled in between licks.

"I won't!" I screamed. "I'm sorry Clyde, please stop, I'm sorry!" I screamed as I tried to run to the other side of the bed to avoid the vicious lashes from his belt. He grabbed me, threw down the belt and started yanking off my ball gown, then threw me onto the bed on my stomach.

He pinned me down to the bed with his weight, yanked off my panties, and forced his manhood in between my buttocks, I screamed in pain.

"You are mine, how many times must I keep reminding you?" He yelled.

I screamed and screamed as he thrust faster and faster until he finally climaxed. He got up and gave me a look of disgust. Then he walked into the bathroom. I could hear the shower turn on. A few minutes later he came out of the shower and put his tuxedo back on. He went into the closet and after a few seconds, he walked back out into the bedroom. I noticed that he was holding his gun in his hand. He walked over to the bed, sat down and grabbed my chin, pointing the gun at my forehead. My heart dropped. Was he going to shoot me?

"If you ever think about leaving me for another man, I will kill you," he said softly. Then he stood up and walked out of the room without saying another word. A few minutes later I heard his truck pull off.

After Clyde left, I dialed Linda's number. I could not take this abuse any longer.

"Hello?" Linda answered in a sleepy voice.

"Linda, please come and get me." I sobbed into the phone.

"Karen, what's wrong honey!" She asked. I could not even respond I started crying even harder.

"I am on my way!" Linda yelled and promptly hung up the phone. She must have been speeding because a ride that should have taken forty-five minutes, only took her twenty, when I opened the front door, she took one look at me and gasped.

"Come on Karen, let's get out of here," she said as she pulled me by the hand and led me to her car.

"I should take you to the hospital," she said with a look of concern on her face. It was obvious that she must have been in the bed when I called because she still had on her pajamas and bedroom slippers, she also had soft sponge rollers in her hair and a pink and yellow scarf tied around her head.

"No, No, I am okay; just take me to your house." I said in between sobs. When we pulled up to her house, all the lights were out.

"Where are your parents?" I asked.

"They are on a two-week vacation in Florida. They just left yesterday," she replied as she got out of the car. When we walked into the house I went straight to her bathroom. I looked in the mirror and almost fainted.

Both of my eyes were black and swollen. My lips were the size of grapefruits, and blood was dripping from my nose. I just started crying all over again. Linda walked into the bathroom and hugged me.

"Karen, you have got to get away from him before he kills you," she said as she wiped my nose with a warm washcloth.

"That bastard is crazy, what made him beat you like this? I thought he was taking you to the police ball tonight."

"He did take me, and everything was fine until that guy you and I met at Lazarus last week, showed up at the ball." I sat down on the toilet seat. I had to sit slowly; I was in so much pain from where Clyde had sodomized me. I told her about the events of the night. I also broke down and told Linda the truth about what had put me in the hospital so long ago.

"What am I supposed to do? He is my husband and I made vows before God, for better or worse." I said crying.

"Karen, God does not want you to be abused. He does not expect you to stay in an abusive relationship," she sighed.

"Can I just sleep here tonight?" "I don't want to go home right now."

"Sure," she said with a smile. Linda handed me one of her nightgowns and I went to the spare bedroom, undressed, and laid down. A few hours later, I heard the doorbell.

I could hear Linda yelling at someone so I got up and opened the bedroom door.

"She is not going anywhere!" I heard Linda scream.

"Mind your own business Linda. Karen is my wife and she is going home."

Clyde yelled. I did not want to cause Linda any problems so I put my clothes back on, opened the bedroom door and began walking very slowly down the steps to the living room.

"That's okay Linda. I will go with him." I said in a weak voice as I walked down the last few steps.

"Karen, you do not have to go anywhere with that bastard! There is no reason for him to be putting his hands on you!" She yelled as she put her hands on her hips, and gave Clyde a mean stare.

"Come on Karen, let's go." Clyde said as he walked out of the house. I hugged Linda and followed Clyde out the front door.

"I will call you later Linda." I said then I got inside the truck.

"I am sorry, about tonight Karen." Clyde said as he drove home.

"When I saw that man touching you, I just lost my head." "I can't stand the thought of another man touching you, I love you so much. Please forgive me." I could see he was crying. I did not say anything. I was just too exhausted. When we got home, I went straight to our bedroom and went to bed.

CHAPTER 7

It had been six months since the police ball. For the first few weeks after that night, he was very kind to me. Bringing me flowers home and taking me out. Unfortunately, that treatment did not last long, things went back to normal and the beatings started again.

One morning I got up and felt nauseated. I barely made it to the bathroom before I started vomiting. I knew what was wrong before I even made an appointment to see the doctor. Clyde took me to my doctor's appointment, and my suspicions were correct. I was pregnant. Clyde was so happy. He started drilling me about making sure that I took good care of myself. He told me I had better not have another miscarriage or there would be hell to pay. Chills went down my spine when I thought about the beating he had given me the last time I had a miscarriage.

That evening after my appointment, I received a phone call from Linda. Clyde had left saying that he had to work over and would not be home until the next morning, this was the third time this week he had to work two shifts.

"Karen, Clyde has been seeing another woman," Linda said abruptly. For some reason, her words did not shock me.

"I was out with my friends at a hotel party last night in Dayton, when I saw him with another woman at the same hotel, I ducked into the bathroom so that he would not see me. He was laughing and hugging, kissing her, and feeling on her in front of everyone in the hotel. After they got on the elevator, I went over to the front desk to see if he had a room and sure enough he did," she said. I could hear how upset she was.

"I figured as much. Some one has been hanging up on me when I answer the telephone, Clyde has also been telling me that he has had to do a lot of over time.

Sometimes he does not come home until late the next afternoon." I said with a sigh.

Having another woman never seemed to stop him from wanting to have sex with me.

"I just found out today that I am pregnant again." I whispered into the phone.

"Karen, you have got to get away from him. That man is no good for you, I have a friend who runs a domestic violence shelter in Cleveland, Ohio, If I call her, I know she can help you."

"Thanks Linda, but I am tired right now, can I call you back later?" I needed time to think about everything, I hung up the phone and went into the living room. I sat down on our couch, picked up the remote control, and turned on the television. I was flipping through the channels when a preacher caught my attention.

"God knows all the pain and suffering you have been through; he has seen your tears. You need to put your trust in him and step out on faith. Watch him move mountains in your life." The preacher said to the congregation.

"There will be times in your life when you don't know what to do or which way to turn. There will be people in your life that seem like they are there just to hurt you, but if you put your trust in God, he can remove these people from your life. God can give you a brand-new start." The preacher said with passion.

"You have to put it in God's hands. You may be afraid to do the one thing that you know you need to do to change your situation, but fear is not of God. God gives you courage. Take a step of faith toward happiness, peace, love, and prosperity. God will give you peace, mercy and grace." Members of the congregation were yelling, as the preacher continued with his sermon.

"If you take one step, the Lord will take two. Just trust him, believe that he loves you and he knows your needs. All you have to do is talk to him in prayer." I felt like the preacher was talking to me. It is as if God sent him to speak to me directly. I turned the television off and just sat there for a few minutes. I promised Grandma Ellis and my mother that I would never allow my child to go through the abuse that I experienced. If Clyde had no problem with beating me, what would stop him from mistreating our children? I got on my knees, closed my eyes, and started praying.

"God, the pastor said that if I trust you and take a step in faith, you would protect me. My life until now has not been a happy one. I have gone through so much, from childhood up until now, I want happiness God, I want peace. So if I leave Clyde, you have to take care of me and my unborn child, you have to provide for us, your word cannot lie. The bible says that if I have faith even as small as a mustard seed, nothing will be impossible to me. I need your help lord. Please deliver me from my torture, and give me a new life, a better life. I pray for this in Jesus name amen." I got up off my knees and sat on the couch. I started crying and rocking back and forth.

"Grandma Ellis said that you hear all prayers, God I pray you heard mine." I said in between sobs, after a while, I got up and started turning off the lights to go to bed when the telephone rang, I walked back over to the table and picked up the phone.

"Hello?" I answered.

"Hello Karen, its Linda. I just talked with my friend in Cleveland and she said if you come tonight, she has a spot available for you." I figured this had to be my sign from God, he had heard my prayers.

"Okay, I will be ready in an hour," I replied.

"You are really willing to leave tonight?" I could tell she was surprised that I had actually said I would go.

"'It's time for me to leave Clyde, if I am going to do it; I have to do it right now." I sighed.

"Okay, I will be there to get you in an hour."

Linda arrived at my house exactly one hour later. When she arrived, she helped me to put my bags and suitcases in her trunk. I quickly locked the front door and got into the car. I was so nervous. I kept thinking Clyde was going to pull up behind us and pull a gun on me, demanding that I get out of the car. I did not start to relax until we were on 71 north and had left Columbus.

"How far along did the doctor say you were?" Linda asked.

"The doctor said I am two and a half months pregnant." I answered, staring out the window.

"You know you did the right thing don't you?" Linda said glancing at me.

"Yes. I prayed about it and I feel like God was telling me that I needed to leave."

"My friend told me that they help women like you get away from their abusers and start new lives." Linda said as she lit a cigarette. She glanced at me, and then promptly put the cigarette out in the ashtray.

"Is it a dirty place?" I asked. I had seen the shelters in downtown Columbus.

They were not very pretty; there were always drunks and dirty looking homeless people standing in front of them.

"I don't know, but at least it's a start," she said glancing at me as she drove. At some point during the ride I must have fallen asleep. When I woke up, I saw signs saying Cleveland. I had never been out of Columbus. This was really going to be a new experience for me. When Linda realized that I was awake she gave me a warm smile.

"I told my dad what was going on and he told me to give this to you," she handed me a white envelope, I opened it and pulled out a wad of bills. My eyes grew large as I started counting the money that was inside.

"My dad said he put five thousand dollars in there. He told me to tell you to purchase a car and to use the rest for your apartment. He also told me to tell you that if you ever needed more money not to hesitate to call him." I could not believe it. Her dad was always nice to me. I do not know what I would have done without Linda and her parents.

"My friend's name is Samantha; she is a very nice person, I have been dating her brother for about six months, you will meet her tonight."

"Thank you so much Linda." I said with tears in my eyes.

"There is no need to thank me. You have always been like a sister to me. What good is it to have family if they can't be there when you really need them?" She said smiling. I could see tears rolling down her face. Linda had never been one to show too much emotion, when we were little, if she ever got in trouble by our grandmother, she would hide in a closet or a bedroom so that none of her cousins could see her cry.

"I will be calling to check up on you," she said sniffing. She reached into her glove compartment and pulled out a tissue box. After handing me a few tissues, she began wiping her own face.

"I love you Karen," she said gently patting me on my thigh. I did not realize it at the time, but that would be the last time I would ever see Linda.

CHAPTER 8

The Shelter was located far out in the suburbs of Cleveland, Ohio. It looked nothing like the shelters I had seen in Columbus. In fact it was a very beautiful and large, Victorian brick house. The house was located on a large acre of land. There were beautiful flowers and small lights that lined the long walkway to the front door. There were no signs indicating that it was a shelter. There was a van and three cars parked in the long driveway leading to the two car garage.

"I will help you carry your bags." Linda said as she turned off the ignition. The nearest house seemed like it was a few blocks away. It was so beautiful. The night air was warm, and the moon seemed to be shining brighter than normal. I helped Linda carry my bags up the walkway to the French doors.

"Are you ready?" Linda asked smiling.

"As ready as I am going to get." I replied with a sigh. I took a deep breath as Linda rung the doorbell.

A few seconds later a young woman opened the door,

"Hello Linda, I am so glad you made it here safely. Did you have any problems finding it?" The woman asked.

"Hello Samantha, it's good to see you again. No, I did not have any problems."

"This is my cousin Karen King." Linda said pointing toward me.

Samantha looked like she may have been in her middle to late twenties. She was a very petite woman with long brown hair, caramel colored skin, and a very pretty smile.

"Hello Karen, I am so glad you decided to come." She said as she held her hand out to me.

"Thank you." I said shyly as I shook her hand. She led us to a large room beside the front door. The room had beautiful flowers; there was a large sectional couch and pictures of women and children hanging on the walls.

"You can place your bags in here for right now, follow me to my office." I never dreamed that they had shelters that looked like this. Linda and I followed Samantha down a long hallway past another room. It was a large living room with leather furniture and a big screen TV. There were three women sitting on the couch and some children playing in the middle of the floor. Next to the living room was her office.

"Please sit down." Samantha said pointing toward two seats next to her desk.

"I need to ask you a few questions and have you fill out some paper work." She said as she started shifting through the piles of papers on her desk.

"Okay." I replied as Linda and I sat down.

"Are you married?"

"Yes." I answered.

"Do you have any children or are you pregnant?"

"I am two and a half months' pregnant." I replied nervously.

"We have a doctor who makes visits on Thursdays; I will put you on the list, you will receive vitamins and prenatal checkups while you are here," She said as she wrote my name on a sheet of paper attached to a clipboard.

"Now tell me a little about your husband and the abuse you have been experiencing." We sat in the office for about an hour as I told her about Clyde, it was a little difficult for me to talk about everything I had gone through, I started crying.

Samantha was very understanding and gave me a lot of comfort, she handed me a Kleenex and patted my arm telling me everything was going to be okay.

"Let me tell you a little about our program," she said as she sat back in her chair and crossed her legs, pulling her skirt down over her knees. "This facility only houses women for four weeks. During their stay here, we try to help them find employment and apartments to live in. We also have what we call transitional housing. We own eight houses; they are located in Georgia, New York, and California. We send pregnant women and women in very dangerous situations to those houses. Because you are pregnant, you will be sent to one of those houses." She paused, and looked at some paperwork on her desk.

"We have an opening in Atlanta, Georgia. Would you agree to go to Georgia?" She asked. I looked at Linda; I had never been out of Columbus, let alone out of Ohio. I was not sure I would be able to make such a drastic move and go to a place where I did not know anyone.

Linda must have been reading my mind because she looked at me and took a hold of my hand.

"Karen, I know that this may seem very scary, but you must know that you need to get away. You cannot go back to Columbus, if Clyde finds you; you will be going back through the same thing all over again. This program helps women get out of bad situations and get back on their feet. Besides, I will be here for you whenever you need me," she said patting my hand. Linda always knew the right things to say; she always knew how to make me feel better.

"Yes I will go." I said slowly. I knew I would just have to trust God. I knew that he had not brought me this far to leave me.

"Good, all the paperwork will be completed and you will be leaving with two other ladies from the shelter in two weeks."

"Linda told me that you would be purchasing a car. We have a car lot that we use. We will assist you in getting a car and tags before you leave so that you will be able to drive your own car to Atlanta. When our van leaves for Georgia, you will be following them in your car. The transitional program in Atlanta will assist you with whatever you need. Once you have your baby, they will assist you with getting into school, or getting back into the job market. We work with many different companies and programs in Georgia."

"I would love to go back to school, I was in nursing school, but my husband forced me to leave." I said. I was starting to feel like this was going to all work out.

We talked for a little longer, and then she had me fill out a lot of paperwork.

"Do either of you have any questions?" Samantha asked as she stapled my paperwork together and put them in a file.

"Will Linda be able to call me here?" I asked. I needed to be able to keep in touch with someone from my family.

"No, she will not be allowed to call. For security reasons, no one is given the number to the shelter, usually, we do not even allow outsiders to bring the women in, generally, the police escort the women here, but I made an exception.

A domestic violence shelter is similar to what was called the Underground Rail Road back in slavery time, it is important that the shelter's location stay confidential for the safety of the women. Linda will be allowed to write to this P.O. Box address."

Samantha handed me and Linda each a business card with the P.O. Box address written on it.

"Phones can be tapped and traced. You said your husband is a police officer, it would be easy for him to have Linda's telephones tapped, you should correspond only by mail, but if you need to call you must do so outside of the facility."

"I never knew that domestic violence shelters existed." I said staring at the business card she had just given me. I was trying to absorb all the changes that were taking place in my life.

"There are domestic violence shelters all over the United States. However a lot of shelters have had to close down due to the decrease of government funding." Samantha replied.

"Well, I have to get ready to go I have a long ride back to Columbus and I have to be at work at 8:30 in the morning." Linda said as she got up from her chair.

I stood up with her and gave her a big hug. I could feel tears starting to form in my eyes.

"Thank you Linda for all you have done, thank you for being there for me."

"No problem, I just want you and your baby to be safe," she said and kissed me softly on the cheek. I walked Linda back out to her car. I stood there waving like a little girl as she pulled off. I felt heaviness in my chest as I watched her car drive away. I was really going to miss her, but at least we would be able to write to each other.

After Linda left, Samantha gave me a tour of the rest of the house. Then she took me to the living room so that she could introduce me to some of the women.

"Ladies we have a new resident, her name is Karen King." Samantha announced as we entered the room.

"This is Tina." Samantha said pointing to a young black girl sitting at a computer. She appeared to be about 18 years old, if that old.

"What's up," Tina did not bother looking up from the computer, just raised her hand in acknowledgment.

"Hello Tina." I replied.

"This is Monica," Samantha stated as she pointed to a young Puerto Rican woman who was sitting on the couch.

"Hello Monica." I said waving my hand.

"Hello Karen." Monica had a very deep accent. I liked how she said my name.

"This is Charlotte." Samantha said pointing to a Caucasian woman who was sitting next to Monica on the couch, She had a long sheet draped over her shoulder and was breast-feeding her baby.

"Hello Charlotte." I said with a smile.

"Hello." Charlotte replied as she pulled the sheet that she had covering her baby up a little farther on her shoulder as her infant continued to eat.

"All the other ladies are in their rooms. You will meet them at the meeting tomorrow night. Come on lets go grab your bags and I will show you to your room." Samantha said as she left the room.

"Okay." I replied following her like a puppy.

We went back into the sitting room and picked up my bags. As we were walking up the stairs, three children came running past us. One of the children almost slipped and fell.

"Tom, Janet, and Kim, what have I told you about running in the house? Go find a seat right now!" Samantha ordered.

"Yes ma'am." The children said as they walked slowly down the last few steps. Samantha and I walked up the remaining steps and past three sets of doors. She finally stopped and knocked on a door.

"Come in," someone answered from the other side. Samantha opened the door, and walked in, I followed her.

"Jessica, this is your new roommate. Her name is Karen King." Samantha turned toward me. "Jessica has three children that also share this room with her."

"Hello Karen." Jessica greeted me with a smile.

"Hello. It's nice to meet you." I replied.

"Your room is attached to Jessica's," Samantha said while pointing to an adjoining room.

"You should find all your linen and towels in the bedroom closet. You are responsible for making sure that your towels and linen stay clean. You can use the laundry room at any time as long as it is before 9:00pm. We will provide all of your laundry supplies." Samantha said walking toward my new room.

"You will find some sanitary supplies and personal care items in the top drawer.

If you run out of personal supplies, just ask whatever office worker is on duty to get you some, there are two sets of bathrooms on this floor. All the women in the house share those two bathrooms, every woman in the house also has chores. Everyone must help keep the house clean. Each week the chores are rotated and a new list is put up on my office door, make sure that you check the list in the morning because I will be adding your name to it." Samantha said as she walked back toward the door.

"Okay," I said as I scooted my bags toward the adjoining room.

"Breakfast is at 8:30 a.m. Lunch is at 1:00p.m. and dinner is at 6:30 p.m.

Everyone must be on time for meals. If you are not down stairs before prayer, you will not be permitted to eat breakfast. Curfew is at 6:00pm. If you miss curfew more than twice you will be released from the facility."

"Okay." I replied. I guess it was necessary to have rules so that the house would run smoothly.

"I will see you ladies tomorrow evening. My shift is over. If you need anything just ask the night shift attendant, her name is Mrs. Sanford."

"Good night." Jessica and I said at the same time.

"Your room has a door with a lock on it in case you need privacy" Jessica stated as she took braids out of her daughter's hair. Jessica appeared to be in her late twenty's or early thirty's. She was a light-skinned woman with freckles and short, red, curly hair.

Her fingernails and toenails were neatly manicured, and her eyebrows arched. I could tell that she was a woman who took great pains in keeping up her appearance, her daughter appeared to be the splitting image of her mother.

"Thank you." I walked to the adjoining room and started unpacking my bags. A little girl came up to me. She had plated braids and big brown eyes.

"What's your name?" She asked as she sat down on my bed.

"My name is Karen, what's yours?" I asked as I started pulling clothes out of my suitcase.

"Tamika, I am six years old, I just had a big birthday party," she said with a huge smile.

"Well that's very nice Tamika." I replied as I began hanging up my clothes in the closet.

"That's my sister Tammy in there with mommy. She hates getting her hair done.

She is ten years old, my brothers' name is Tom, and he is twelve years old. He is downstairs playing with his friends, I don't like Tom because he always calls me a bighead." Tamika said as she hopped up and down on my bed. I figured Tom must have been one of the children that ran past me and Samantha on our way up the steps. Before I could reply, I heard Jessica call for her daughter.

"Tamika! Get back in here and let the lady rest."

"Bye." Tamika said with a disappointed look on her face.

"I will see you tomorrow, nice meeting you Tamika." I replied with a smile. Tamika got up and walked to the door. She was a very beautiful little girl. She must have looked more like her father because she did not resemble her mother or her big sister. She was darker than they were and unlike her mother and her sister, she had jet-black hair.

"Do you want me to close your door?" She asked.

"Yes, I am about to go to bed." I said as I pulled out my nightgown. Without another word, Tamika walked out the door and closed it behind her. I was so exhausted, so much had happened in the last twenty-four hours. I finished putting away my clothes, put on my nightgown, said my prayers and went to bed.

CHAPTER 9

The next morning I woke up to the sound of children playing. I glanced at my watch it was 7:30am. I got up and put on my bathrobe and house slippers, picked up the bag of personal supplies that the shelter had given me and opened my bedroom door.

"Good morning." I said as I walked into Jessica's portion of the room.

"Good morning, how did you sleep last night? I hope the kids didn't keep you awake." Jessica and her children were already fully dressed.

"I slept like a baby, I didn't hear a thing." I said as I walked out of our bedroom.

I went to the bathroom and knocked on the door.

"I will be out in a minute," a female voice answered. I decided to wait outside the door until she was finished. I watched as women and children walked down the hallway. A short heavyset woman walked up to me.

"Are you waiting to get in the bathroom?"

"Yes." I replied.

"The other bathroom at the end of the hallway is empty," she said pointing to the bathroom past the staircase.

"Thanks," I replied. I took a long hot shower; the water felt so good, I stood still and let it beat on my back and neck.

When the water started getting cold, I got out, put my clothes on, and went downstairs to the dining room.

The room was crowded; there were about thirty women and children, sitting at the dining room table.

"Here's a free seat over here." The Puerto-Rican woman named Monica yelled from across the room, I recognized her from last night. I walked over to the seat next to her and sat down.

"So where are you from?" She asked. Everyone was talking so loud and she had such a strong accent; I almost did not understand what she said.

"I am from Columbus, Ohio. Where are you from?" I asked.

"I'm originally from Puerto- Rico, but I was raised in New York."

"I have always lived in Columbus, this is the first time I have ever left."

"So, you are going to Atlanta too?" She asked as she glanced around the room.

"Yes, how did you know?" I asked with raised eyebrows.

"Samantha told me. My children and I are going also."

"Have you ever been there before?" I asked. I felt a little better; at least I would not be completely alone.

"No, but I heard that it's real nice."

The cooks were setting up the breakfast buffet. I watched as they brought out a big tub of bacon.

"Okay everyone; let's have a moment of silence before prayer," an older woman stated as she stood up from the table.

"Everyone please stand up and hold the hand of the person standing next to you." She said smiling. Everyone stood up, children and adults began holding hands. we formed a big circle around the dining room table.

"Who would like to say prayer this morning?"

"I will," an older black woman volunteered.

"Thank you Lord for allowing us to wake up this morning in safety, thank you for the food that we are about to consume. Please watch over each and every one of us, as we begin this new day. Amen."

"Amen," everyone said at the same time.

"For any new people that came in last night or early this morning, my name is Ms. Hanford, I am the daytime house manager. Enjoy your breakfast." Ms.Hanford said as she walked over to the buffet table. She reminded me of my grandmother, she was heavy set and short with age lines across her forehead. It was obvious that she was not the type to miss breakfast or any other meal for that matter.

Women and children followed suit and started heading toward the buffet table where there were paper plates, forks, cups and napkins. After I made my plate I sat down and started eating. I listened as different women talked about their plans for the day. The breakfast was delicious, I had chosen fresh fruit, eggs, bacon and toast. Monica had only fresh fruit, toast, and eggs on her plate, I noticed that her two children were also only eating fruit, toast, and eggs.

"You should try this bacon, it's delicious." I stated as I stuffed a long strip of bacon into my mouth. I was starving; I had not eaten since yesterday at about lunchtime.

"We do not eat pork; it's not good for you," she said as she took a bite of her eggs. "It isn't?" I asked. I glanced at the bacon left on my plate. I had been eating bacon all my life, It might not be good for me, but it sure tasted good. After breakfast, the woman named Ms. Hanford stood up again.

"The meeting this evening will begin promptly at 8:00pm in the conference room. I need to see the following people in my office after chores are completed." She stated as she pulled a piece of paper out of her pocket.

"Karen King, Monica Lopez, and Jessica Smith, everyone else have a productive day," Everyone got up and started doing their chores. I went to the office door to see what my chores for the week would be, I looked down the list until I found my name.

My chore was to wipe off the dining room table for breakfast, lunch and dinner. I walked back into the dining room, a woman and her children were throwing away paper plates, cups and utensils into a big trash can. I walked past them into the kitchen.

"Excuse me," I said to one of the cooks. "Can you please tell me where to locate the supplies I need to clean the dining room table?"

"Sure honey," the cook said and handed me a bucket, some disinfectant, and a cloth.

"Thanks," I replied.

"No problem, just make sure you clean the bucket and clothe out when you are finished and put it back in this closet, I use those to clean up the kitchen." After I cleaned off the table and put everything away, I started walking toward Ms. Hanford's office.

Monica and my roommate Jessica were already seated inside Ms. Hanford's office when I walked through the door.

"Okay, you three ladies will be leaving for Atlanta next Thursday at 6:00am. Monica and Jessica, since you do not have cars you will be riding in the van." Ms Hanford said before turning toward me.

"Karen, Mrs. Jones, who is a volunteer, will be coming to get you today after lunch to take you to the car lot. She should be here by 2:00pm, please be ready and make sure that you have your money. You also have an appt to see Dr. Lewis, Thursday at 10:00a.m. She usually gets here a little early, so make sure you are down stairs no later than 9:30a.m."

"Okay, I replied."

"The three of you will be staying at The Love House, It's about a forty-five minute drive from downtown Atlanta, are there any questions?" We all said no.

"I would like to welcome you Ms. King, we are glad to have you with us, even if it will be for a very short period. You have just taken one of the biggest steps in your life, but I guarantee you will never regret your decision." she turned toward Jessica.

"Please do not leave yet Jessica; I have a few papers I need for you to sign.

Monica and Karen, you may leave, have a good day." Monica and I stood up and walked out of the room.

Mrs. Jones came right after lunch chores and took me to the car lot. I was not sure what to get, but the sales man was very nice and helped me pick out a 1980 red Buick Regal.

"We will have the car serviced at our shop." Mrs. Jones stated.

After we left the car lot, Mrs. Jones took me to get plates for the car and some car insurance. I was so excited; this was my very first car. I had gotten my drivers license when I turned eighteen, but I never had enough money to buy a car.

That night at 8:00pm, the conference room was full. There were about twenty women, all the children were in the playroom with two volunteers. During the meeting I didn't say anything, I just listened as some of the women stood up and told stories of their abuse, after listening to their stories, I realized that I was not alone, each woman in that room had one thing in common, we were all running away from abuse. I learned that domestic violence occurs not only between husband and wife, or boyfriend and girlfriend, but between mother and daughter and father and son. Not all domestic violence is physical; sometimes it is also mental, emotional, or sexual. One thing was for sure, domestic violence was all about one person trying to control and manipulate another human being.

The night before I was to leave Ohio, I received a letter from Linda. She let me know that Clyde had come to see her and was threatening her, demanding that she tell him where I was because I was pregnant with his child. She said she told him that I had called her and told her

I was leaving town but that I did not tell her where I was going. She said he had also been over to my grandmother's house. I wrote her back and let her know that I was leaving Ohio the next morning and that I would write to her once I was settled in Atlanta. I mailed the letter, and then went to bed. Tomorrow was going to be a new beginning for my unborn child and me.

The sound of someone knocking on our bedroom door awakened me the next morning. I turned on my bedside lamp and looked at my watch. It was 4:30a.m, I heard a thump in the next room as Jessica got up to answer the door.

"Good mor ning." I heard Samantha whisper.

"It's time for you ladies to start getting ready; there is cereal, donuts, and coffee in the dining room." Then I heard the door close. Jessica walked over to my room.

"Karen, it's time to get up."

"I'm awake." I said as I sat on the side of my bed and started rubbing my eyes. I had packed all of my bags the night before and had laid out my clothing. I pulled out the pictures of my mother and Grandma Ellis.

"Well you guys, I am on my way to Atlanta, Georgia. I do not know what God has in store for me but I know that you two are watching over me." I whispered. I kissed both pictures and put them back in my suitcase. I put on my bathrobe and walked to the adjoining room.

"Are you ready for our trip?" I asked Jessica. She was in the process of pulling out her children's clothes.

"I use to live in Atlanta." Jessica stated as she pulled out two pairs of socks from her suitcase.

"I met my husband while I was a student at Spellman University. He was a student at Morehouse. I am originally from Savannah, Georgia.

My husband was from California. We moved to Cleveland, Ohio when he got a job here as a computer programmer."

"That's cool, so you already know your way around, do you mind showing me around?" I asked as I walked to the bedroom door.

"Sure, if you don't mind driving me around," we both started laughing. I walked to the bathroom and took a long hot shower. When I finished I stood in front of the mirror naked and put my hands over my stomach. I only had a small pouch; no one could even tell that I was pregnant. Ever since I had started taking the prenatal vitamins the shelters doctor had given me, my morning sickness had disappeared. It was hard to believe that in just six and a half months I would be a mother. "God please let me be able to provide a happy, loving, safe, and peaceful life for my child." I prayed aloud. I finished getting dressed and went down to the dining room. Monica was already making some cereal for her two children.

"Good morning." I said as I walked over to the table and poured myself a glass of orange juice.

"Good morning, I could not sleep all night, I have never been to Georgia before, I hope that it's nice," she said as she sat down at the table next to her two children.

Monica's children looked more like African Americans than Puerto-Ricans. I figured her husband must have been black.

"Me too, Jessica said that she use to live in Atlanta, at least one of us will know our way around." I said as I sat down at the table next to her son.

"I am so glad that we will all be staying at the same house. At least we will know each other and can help each other out.

It's scary, moving to a place where you don't have any family and don't know anyone."

She said as she took a bite of her donut. A few minutes later Jessica and her three children joined us at the table.

"How long do you think it will take us to get there?" I asked Jessica as she sat down across from me.

"Well depending on how fast we drive probably about twelve hours. We should get there between 6:30 and 7:00 tonight." She said as she took a bite of her cereal.

"I have never driven out of town before, I pray I don't lose you guys and get lost." I said with a frown.

"They know that you are not use to driving. I know that they will not go too fast, anyway, it's really a straight shot. Once we get on 71 south, it will take us all the way to 75 south, which will take, us right into Atlanta. You will not get lost." Jessica said smiling. After breakfast, I loaded all of my things into my car. The other women loaded their belongings into a big yellow van. It was 6:00am and we were all ready to go. Samantha came over to me and gave me a big hug.

"I will call Linda for you and let her know that you have left," Samantha stated. I could see tears forming in her eyes. It's funny how easy it is to become attached to people that you have only known for a short time.

"Thank you Samantha for everything, I will never forget you," she smiled then walked over to the van. After saying goodbye to the other women, she told the van driver that we were ready to leave.

As we drove back through Columbus, I felt slightly apprehensive. I made sure that I did not speed, the last thing I needed was to be stopped by the police. Once we crossed over the bridge that connects Ohio with Kentucky I started feeling much better.

"Goodbye Ohio, Goodbye Clyde". I said with a big grin on my face.

A NEW BEGINNING

PART III

Where can I go to get shelter from my storm?

Where is the place that will keep me safe from harm?

Where can I go to escape my crazy spouse?

Someone said I can go to, 'The Love House.'

In this house there are women just like you and me.

Women who are running away from abuse and misery.

CHAPTER 10

After twelve hours of driving and three stops, we finally made it to Atlanta at about 6:00pm that evening. I was amazed at what I saw; downtown Atlanta was so big and beautiful with all its flashing lights. 75 south was packed with drivers anxious to get home after a long day at work. It was the middle of July, the weather was hot yet felt beautiful, and there was not even one cloud in the sky. Even though I was very tired from all the driving, I felt a sense of peace that I had never felt before. We were in bumper-to-bumper traffic. I had never seen a passenger train before, I watched as the train passed by. I turned the radio stations until I came across a Christian channel. The words to the song seemed to jump out at me as the singers sang the words, "Glory to God, for he has brought us a mighty long way." I followed the van as it got onto 20 east. We drove for another forty minutes before finally getting off the freeway. Then we drove another twenty minutes before we finally stopped. We were in a residential neighborhood; these houses looked even nicer than the one I had just left.

'The Love House,' was back off the road, hidden by trees. We drove down a long driveway to the garage. The van door opened and five anxious children jumped out. The children started running around and chasing each other on the front lawn. I was so exhausted, I did not know if I even had the strength to get out of the car. I sat there for a moment and watched Monica and Jessica unloading their things out of the van. After a few minutes, I finally got out of the car and walked to the front door.

There was a well-dressed woman standing in the doorway waiting to greet us. She appeared to be in her late forty's or early fifty's. The one thing that I noticed instantly was that she had a beautiful smile.

Somehow, she reminded me of my mother. She was a slender woman dressed in a pink business suit. She had long black hair that was neatly curled.

"Hello ladies, my name is Mrs. Francis please come in." We all entered the house and followed her to a nicely decorated living room. There were three other women sitting on the couch. Mrs. Francis turned to the children.

"There is a big back yard with swings and slides, you children go out and play with the other kids while your mothers take care of some business." All the children ran toward the direction that Mrs. Francis was pointing to. "Okay ladies, please take a seat. I know you are probably tired from your trip. However, there are a few things that I need to cover with you." We found empty chairs and sat down. The room had two sets of living room furniture, a big screen TV and an aquarium. Mrs. Francis sat in a large brown leather chair, gently crossed her legs, and gave us all a warm smile.

"As I stated earlier, my name is Mrs. Francis, I am the mother and manager of this house. I have been working here for the last twelve years. There are also two other women who assist me. You will meet them later.

Okay, let us start with the introductions. The ladies who have already been here will start first and then we will make our way around," she pointed in a clockwise fashion. "We will start with you, please stand up, state your name, where you are from, how long you have been here, and a little about the situation that brought you to The Love House." A white woman with long hair and glasses stood up.

"My name is Rita Lowe, I am 30 years old. I have five children, two boys and three girls, I have been here for four months. I am originally from Chicago,

Illinois. My husband was a prominent executive in Chicago. I am here at "The Love House," because my husband hired someone to kill me. The man shot at me, three times, five months ago. It is only by the grace of God that only one of the bullets hit me in the shoulder. The police caught the hit man, after he confessed he told the police that my husband had hired him. My husband is on the run and the authorities have not been able to catch him yet. I was sent to the shelter in Cleveland first and then here." After she finished she sat down. A Mexican woman that was sitting next to her stood up.

"My name is Melissa Santiago. I am 36 years old and I have three children. Two girls and a boy, I have been here at "The Love House" for two months. I am originally from Mexico, but my family moved to Monterey, California when I was ten years old. I am here because I left my abusive boyfriend. He is the father of my last two children. I tried to leave him before but he started stalking me and threatening my children. I was sent here from the shelter in California," she quickly sat down. The next woman stood up, she looked like she was still a teenager.

"My name is Kiesha Adams, I am 19 years old and I have one little boy his name is James, he is two years old. I am originally from Detroit, Michigan. I have been at The Love House for six months. I was a prostitute and nightclub dancer in Michigan. After I got pregnant and had my son, I decided I did not want to do it anymore. I tried to walk away, but my pimp, who was also my boyfriend, told me that the only way I could leave the game was in a body bag. He started beating on me and stalking me. He once even pulled a gun on me and threatened to kill me while my son was in the other room.

I was sent to the shelter in Cleveland first, and then here," she quickly sat back down. Out of all the stories, hers seem to touch me the most. She did not look like she was old enough to vote, and had already been on the street turning tricks.

"My name is Jessica Smith. I am 28 years old. I have three children. I am originally from Savannah, Georgia. My husband and I moved to Cleveland, Ohio after he received a job offer at one of the big computer companies. I am here because my ex husband has been stalking me. I found out that he was having an affair with someone at his company, so I divorced him. He refuses to realize that the marriage and the relationship are over. Every time I tried to start my life over in Cleveland, he would show up at my job making threats, or up at my children's school. Since our divorce, he has tried to attack me several times in front of my kids. The shelter thought it would be best if I started my life over in a new state, so they sent me here," she said then sat down. I had never talked with Jessica about her situation; in fact we had never gone into any deep details about our lives. At the meetings in Cleveland, she never talked about her life. Somehow at that moment, I felt closer to her.

Next Monica stood up. My palms started sweating; I knew that I would be the next one to speak.

"My name is Monica Lopez. I have two children a son who is twelve and a daughter who is nine. I am originally from Puerto-Rico. I am here because my ex- husband has raped and tried to kill me several times. Everywhere I go, he finds me. He refuses to let me live my life in peace. He told me that if he cannot have me no one would. I am praying that he does not find me this time." Monica sat down. It was now my turn. I could feel my heart beating fast and my palms sweating as I stood up.

"My name is Karen King. I am 22 years old and I am two and a half months pregnant with my first child. I am from Columbus, Ohio. This is the first time I have ever been outside of my city. I am here because my husband has been raping and beating me since the day we got married. When I found out that I was pregnant I decided it was time to leave. I did not want my child to go through anything like what I went through as a child. Since my husband is a police officer, my cousin thought it was best that I leave the city. The shelter in Cleveland, Ohio said that because I was pregnant I would need a place that I could stay for longer than three or four weeks so they sent me here." I had never spoken aloud like this before about my abuse. I sat back down.

"Well, it seems that all of you have a lot in common and can be a great support system for each other." Mrs. Francis said with a smile.

"I was also once a victim of domestic violence. My first husband beat me so bad that I had to have reconstructive surgery on my face. However, by the grace of God I lived through that experience. I am now happily married to a wonderful man and I have three grown children. The hardest part about starting over is the very beginning. Once you took that first step of faith and said enough is enough, you took the hardest step. Many women never leave their abusers. They make excuses for them, or they blame themselves, or they lie to themselves and say that they cannot make it on their own. Some women have very low self-esteem and figure they cannot do any better or they are just simply scared of being alone. The next step is rebuilding your life.

'The Love House,' is here to help you make the transition from a battered woman to a survivor. Once a month we have a domestic violence meeting at 7:00pm. I think that it's important to have these meeting. It is kind of like a group counseling session.

If there are no questions, I will show you three women to your new rooms so that you can get relaxed," Mrs. Francis stated as she got up from her seat and straightened out her cotton skirt.

"Karen, I will show you to your room first," I followed her down a long hallway.

She opened the door to a small room. "Since you do not have any children with you right now, you will get the room with the single twin bed. Once your baby is born, you will have enough room to put a crib in here. After you have gotten settled come by my office so that you can do your paperwork then you will be finished for the evening. Once again, I want to welcome you to The Love House, and to Atlanta Georgia."

"Thank you." I said as I sat down on the bed. She walked out the door and closed it behind her. I was so exhausted. All I wanted to do was lay down and go to sleep. It had been a very long day. I looked around the room and then went down to Mrs. Francis's office and did my paperwork. Once I was finished, I went out to my car, got out some of my luggage, and then went to my bedroom. I took a quick shower, put on my nightclothes and fell on the bed. All I wanted to do was sleep.

CHAPTER 11

FEBRUARY 19, 1984

I screamed as another massive labor pain tore through my body. I was sweating and feeling faint. I had never experienced pain like this before.

"Just breathe." Monica said as she held my hand rubbing it softly.

"Try to relax." Rita said as she gently rubbed my back. I had been in labor for twenty-two hours; my cervix had only dilated to five cm. The doctors did not want to give me an epidural because they said it would slow down my labor. They were considering doing a C- section. I could hear Jessica and Rita arguing with the nurse.

"Where the hell is the doctor?" Jessica yelled. I could tell she was growing impatient.

"She has been in labor for twenty-two hours, don't you think it's time for them to do something; it's obvious she is in extreme pain." Rita exclaimed.

Jessica was always the hotheaded one. She would lose her patience with you in an instant. Many times over the last few months I had witnessed her tear into someone if she thought they were trying to play her. Rita was always the civil one. She had been the mediator for the women in the house many times when they had gotten into bad arguments and were on the verge of fighting. Monica was the emotional one. She would break down and start crying in a heartbeat.

"Please calm down. The doctor is well aware of Mrs. King's condition." The old Chinese nurse stated as she checked the baby's heartbeat.

"Well where the hell is he?" Jessica yelled.

"Ma'am, you are going to have to calm down or I will have to ask you to leave." The nurse stated sternly, obviously surprised at Jessica's foul language.

"I am going to sue this hospital if they do not come and get this baby out of me!" I yelled after another horrible contraction hit me even harder than the last one. The contractions were coming fast, but for some reason my cervix was not opening as quickly as it should have, I did not feel like I could go through another hour of this pain. The doctor came in, checked me and finally said the words I had been praying to hear.

"Her cervix is not dilating fast enough and the baby's heartbeat is starting to slow down. Get her prepared for a C- section and take her down to room seven," he ordered.

"Thank you Jesus." I said weakly after the next contraction had subsided.

Suddenly, nurses filled the room, Jessica, Rita, and Monica moved to the side so they could do their job. The nurses rushed me to the surgery room; put an IV in my arm and I was given medication that numbed my body. Once the pain stopped, I was so exhausted that I fell asleep. Unfortunately, I was not awake when seven pound six once Kacess'ion Monique King entered the world.

"Mrs. King, Mrs. King." I felt someone nudging me; I slowly opened my eyes to see a young black nurse smiling at me. I was no longer in the surgery room. I was now in my own hospital room. I turned my head to the right and saw Monica and Jessica passed out on the couch. I turned my head to the left and saw Rita passed out on the other chair. They had been there for me during my entire pregnancy. It was as if they had decided to take me under their wings. I was cool with the other women at the house.

However, the friendship that I shared with Rita, Jessica, and Monica was more like a family relationship. They were like sisters to me.

"What time is it?" I asked the nurse. I felt very groggy.

"It's 5:00am." The nurse answered as she checked my vital signs and the dressing on my stomach.

"What did I have?" I asked.

"You had a beautiful seven pound, six once little girl who is very healthy. Would you like to see her?" She asked smiling.

"Yes please." I closed my eyes; I was still feeling very sleepy. I had not had a good nights sleep since the contractions first started two days ago. It seemed like I only had my eyes closed a few seconds when I heard the nurse call my name again. I opened my eyes to see the nurse standing beside me holding a small bundle in her arms. I lifted my arms and took the baby, she was indeed a beauty. She was sleeping peacefully, I could see some of her fathers features already. She had his thick eyebrows and small nose. She had a head full of dark curly hair.

When she yawned, I could see deep dimples in both cheeks. I opened the blanket so that I could count her fingers and toes. I had heard horror stories of children that were born with six fingers on each hand, or only three toes on each foot. I counted ten fingers and ten toes, she was perfect. I could tell that she was going to be much lighter than I was. At first glance, a person would have thought that she belonged to a white mother.

With my dark skin, no one would have guessed I would have had such a light baby. I wanted to hold her longer but I was still feeling very weak and sleepy. The nurse must have sensed it because she reached down and took the baby from me.

"I will put her back in the crib; you will have plenty of time to spend with her later. Right now you need to concentrate on getting all the rest you can." She walked away carrying my greatest accomplishment in her arms.

Later that morning Jessica, Rita and Monica went home. They promised that they would take turns checking up on me until I was released from the hospital.

I decided to give Linda and my grandmother a call. I had not talked with Linda since the day she dropped me off at the shelter. I had been so busy trying to learn my way around Atlanta, I had not even written to her since the night before I left Ohio. First, I dialed Linda's' number, a recorded message said that the number was disconnected.

That was odd; Uncle Jason and Aunt Susie had that same number for as long as I could remember, they never had their telephone number disconnected before. I called my grandmother's house.

"Hello Grandmother." I said when I heard her answer the phone.

"Karen, my goodness girl, where in the heck are you!" I could hear apprehension in her voice.

"I'm fine; I called to tell you that I just had a little girl. I named her Kacess'ion Monique. I tried to call Linda but Uncle Jason's phone is disconnected. Do you have their new number?" I heard her sigh and then she said in a very slow and low voice,

"Karen, Linda is dead. They found her body bruised and stabbed behind a bakery store on Karl road." I could not believe what I was hearing; Grandmother must have been playing some cruel trick on me.

"What!" I screamed, that can't be true, no you are lying."

"Karen!" My grandmother said in a stern voice. I could tell she was surprised that I thought she was lying. "I would never tell a lie like that, someone raped and killed her!" She yelled into the phone. I started crying.

"Did they find out who did it?" I sobbed.

"No, but they are searching for her ex- boyfriend. No one seems to know where he disappeared to." I could hear my grandmother sniffing. I knew she had started crying.

"When she didn't come home from class, her parents started getting worried.

They called the police and put out a search for her. They found her two days later. Whoever killed Linda must have kidnapped her from school because her car was still parked on campus." I started crying harder. I should have been there. I did not even get to go to her funeral and say goodbye.

"Karen, Clyde has been coming by here every week asking me if I have seen you.

He is accusing Linda and me of depriving him of seeing his child. I told him that I had not seen or heard from you in months. Karen where are you? When are you coming home? Everyone has been so worried about you. The only reason that we have not had the police out looking for you is because Linda kept telling us that you were okay."

"I am not coming back to Columbus Grandmother. There is nothing there for me anymore. I am through with Clyde; I don't care if I never see him again." I said as I wiped my eyes with some tissue.

"Karen, Clyde has a right to see his daughter. You cannot just leave your husband. The two of you need to sit down and talk. You need to get your family back together. Your child needs a father and you need your husband, you cannot make it by yourself. I think that you are being very immature and selfish." I was not in the mood to hear what my grandmother had to say. Linda had been right, just because Grandmother stayed in an abusive relationship with my grandfather all those years did not mean that I had to. I felt like I had grown a lot over the last few months. I was not the same scared little girl that I was before I left Ohio.

"I am not returning to Columbus, I have started a new life. This is my life and I will do what I think is best for my daughter and me. Listen Grandmother, I have to go I will call back later." I hung up the phone before she had a chance to reply. I loved my grandmother, but I did not agree with many of her philosophies.

For a long time I tried to do anything and everything I could to make her happy. I always gave her the most respect because I knew that she had taken me in and given me a home.

I sat back on the bed and started crying again. Linda had always been like a sister to me. She was the only person that always went out of her way for me, even when we were young. To think that someone would do something that horrible to her made me nauseous. I cried so long that I cried myself to sleep.

CHAPTER 12

Five days after the birth of my daughter, I was discharged from the hospital. The women at the house had decorated my bedroom and were anxiously awaiting my arrival. I was still distraught over my cousin's murder. I had not been able to eat, and had not said much of anything over the last four days. I was still in a lot of pain from the C-section, but the nurses made sure that I was up and walking within two days of my daughter's birth.

I walked to my room and put Kacess'ion in her crib. Then I walked over to the closet and searched for my photo album. I looked at all the old pictures of Linda and me when we were young. I took out the pictures of us at our prom. That had been such a funny day. Linda had hooked me up with some nerd. He was not cute at all, but since I did not have a date, I could not be choosey. Linda always had men falling all over her. Where as, I did not have any choices, she had a hard time trying to choose. She literally had men fighting over her. On the day of our prom, we rode in separate cars. First, we had dinner at a nice restaurant. After dinner, my date and I were supposed to follow Linda and her date to Embassy Suites. My date said he had to stop at home first because he had forgotten his asthma inhaler. He said he knew his way and would meet them there. After we left his house, the jerk got lost. At first, I thought everything was cool. I did not realize we were lost until I saw signs saying 100 miles to Cincinnati.

That is when he finally admitted that we were lost. I tried to call Uncle Jason's house to get directions but he had already left. By the time we finally found the hotel, we had been driving around in circles for at least two hours. When we arrived at the hotel Linda was angry. She cussed my date out so bad that he started crying right there on the spot. He left the prom early and I ended up tagging behind Linda and her date. Her date was pissed off because he thought he was going to get some late night booty action. Linda let him know that she was not going to leave me. By the end of the night, we were both dateless. We ended up going bowling and to a house party. We still had a lot of fun that night.

I started crying all over again. I was going to miss her so much. I pulled her graduation picture out of the photo album. I put the picture in a small frame and sat it on my dresser next to my mother's picture. Three people that meant the world to me were gone. My mother who died when I was born and who I never got a chance to meet, Grandma Ellis who had loved and nurtured me for the first seven years of my life, and Linda who was my cousin and my best friend.

"Linda, say hello to Grandma Ellis, and my mother for me. I guess now I have three angels watching over my daughter and me.

I walked over to Kacess'ion's crib and picked her up. She looked so peaceful in my arms. I kissed her gently on the forehead. Then I laid her down on my bed so that I could check her diaper. She started to cry so I picked her back up and began breast feeding her. The nurse told me that breast milk was the best milk that I could give my baby. After she was satisfied and had fallen back to sleep, I gently laid her back in her crib. Then I laid down and took a much-needed nap.

I was asleep when someone knocked on the door. Rita stuck her head into my room.

"I'm really sorry to hear about your cousin. I know it is hard when you lose someone you love." She walked over to the crib and gently massaged Kacess'ion's arm.

"Your daughter is so beautiful, do you mind if I hold her?"

"Sure go ahead Rita." I said with a smile.

Rita was the only white friend I ever had. I never considered myself prejudice, it is just that in my neighborhood whites and blacks never hung out together. My friendship with Rita showed me that a person's skin color or race has nothing to do with their personality. I considered Rita to be a very close friend. When I looked at her I did not see a white woman, I saw someone I loved like a sister. Rita reached into the crib and gently picked Kacess'ion up, cradling her in her arms.

"I love children. That is probably why I had so many. It has always been my dream to own a day care center. I hope that one day my dream will come true." She said, stroking Kacess'ions soft curly hair.

"You are so good with children Rita; I know that everyone will want to bring their children to your daycare center. I know I will, Kacess'ion will be your first child." I said with a smile. There was another knock at the door.

"Come in!" I yelled. Mrs. Francis walked into my room. She was holding envelopes in her hand. She walked over to Rita and looked at my daughter.

"How is our new bundle of joy doing?" She asked while gently rubbing Kacess'ion's soft, curly, black hair.

"She is doing fine." I said with a weak smile.

"How about you, how are you doing? I know you have to be really sore."

"I guess I am doing as well as can be expected." I said in a low voice.

Mrs. Francis gave me a quick look; I could see concern in her eyes.

"Is everything okay?" She asked as she came over to the bed and sat down next to me.

"Karen's cousin was murdered two weeks ago in Columbus, Ohio. She is feeling really down, her cousin was the one who helped her get away from her husband." Rita stated as she placed Kacess'ion back into the crib. Sadness filled Mrs. Francis eyes. She reached over and gave me a big hug. I could smell the expensive cologne that she always wore.

"I am so sorry to hear that honey." I started crying again.

"She was not just a cousin, she was my best friend." I could not control the tears; they started flowing down my face like a small river.

"Rita, would you please bring me some Kleenex." Mrs. Francis asked as she patted my thigh.

"Sure." Rita replied as she walked out of my room.

"I know that there is nothing I can say to ease your pain during your time of grief, except to let you know that we are all here for you." Rita walked back into the room and held the tissue box out toward me. I took three tissues and began wiping my nose and my face.

"Thank you Rita." I blew my nose with one of the tissues.

"I just pray that they catch the bastard that killed her." I said staring at the wall. If I could have found the killer myself I would have, he deserves to die. "I stated.

"They haven't found the killer?" Mrs. Francis asked.

"No, but my grandmother thinks it was her ex- boyfriend. She said the police are searching for him. They want to bring him in for questioning." I replied as I tossed the tissues into the wastebasket beside my bed.

"I almost forgot to tell you that you have some mail." Mrs. Francis stated as she handed me the envelopes she had been holding. One of the letters was from the Dekalb Housing Authority; the other was a letter from Linda. The postmark had last months date on it. She must have written it right before she was murdered. I opened the letter from the Housing Authority. I wanted to save Linda's letter to read in private. Once I read the letter from the housing Authority I smiled.

"God is so good; it's a letter telling me that I have been approved for section eight. "My briefing will be in two weeks, March the 2nd at 9:30 in the morning." It had finally arrived. I applied for section eight two days after I arrived in Atlanta.

"Congratulations Karen, I guess you will be leaving us soon. We will assist you in getting second hand furniture from the furniture bank." Mrs. Francis stated.

"Thank you Mrs. Francis." I decided not to tell her that I still had two thousand dollars left from the money that my uncle had given me. I wanted to keep that money for emergencies, and for the deposit for my new place.

"Your welcome dear, well I have to go." Mrs. Francis said as she stood up and walked toward my door.

"Me too, I have to get dinner started. Don't worry about cooking anything for the next week. We are going to cook for you. We know that you need your rest." Rita said as she followed Mrs. Francis out the door.

I stood up, closed my door, and locked it. Then I went over to glance at my daughter. She was truly a blessing from God. I gently ran my hand across her smooth, soft cheek. I decided I wanted to read my letter from Linda. I walked over to the bed and picked up the letter. I sat down on my bed and tore open the envelope, pulled out the letter, and began reading:

Hello Karen, how are you doing? I sure do miss you. From my calculations you should be about eight months pregnant. I have not heard from you, Samantha told me that you would probably not write me for a while. Please send me some pictures when your baby is born. My life has really been crazy lately; someone broke into my parents house last week while we were out of town. The house was a complete mess. My room seemed to be hit the worst. My parents said they are going to move, Mom said she does not feel safe anymore. The police were not able to find any fingerprints. I broke up with this crazy man named John last month. We had been dating for about three months. A few weeks ago, I found out that he was cheating on me. He has been whining and begging me to take him back. You know how I am once I decide that it is over. I had to get a restraining order on him because he started showing up at my job and at my parents house acting crazy and making threats. My dad thinks he is the one who broke into our house. School is going good I just cannot wait to graduate. Well I have to go. Write to me if you can.

Best friends forever,
Love Linda

I held the letter against my heart; it would be the last letter I would ever receive from her.

CHAPTER 13

The next few weeks seemed to pass by quickly. After I went for my section eight briefing, I decided to wait until Kacess'ion and I had our six-week checkups before I started physically going out and looking for a place. I wanted to concentrate on getting a house. Every week I would buy the Atlanta Journal. There was always a large real- estate section in the Sunday paper. It seemed like everyone in Atlanta wanted to lease, sale, or rent his or her home. There also seemed to be a large number of section eight homes available. I had written out all the goals that I wanted to achieve and I gave myself a date. Mrs. Francis told us to start each month with a goal. Then write a list of things we needed to do in that month to help us reach our goal. The one thing that I loved about Mrs. Francis was that she was so classy and so straightforward. She let us know that her goal was to make sure that we could survive on our own once we left. My goal for the month was to find a house. In the briefing, the section eight workers stated that the vouchers were only good for three months.

Each morning I would get up, get me and Kacess'ion dressed, eat breakfast and go to housing appointments. Some of the houses that I went to see were in rough parts of Atlanta. It is not that I had such a big problem with living in a ghetto; my grandmother lived smack dead in the middle of the ghetto in Columbus. However, I knew that ghetto.

I knew where to go and where not to go. I knew that Main Street in Columbus was not a street that I wanted to live on because certain parts were known for prostitution and drugs. I knew that I never wanted to live in the Short North in Columbus because that is where they had a lot of gang activity. I knew Columbus like the back of my hand. I did not know Atlanta. What seemed peaceful and nice during the day, could have been crazy at night.

A few houses were in neighborhoods that were not that bad, but they wanted more than my voucher would pay. If I stayed within the eight hundred dollar mark, I would not have to pay any rent. If I went above eight hundred I would have to pay the rest. Since I did not have a job only a welfare check, I knew that was out of the question.

After two and a half months of searching it seemed as if I would never find a place. I was starting to get depressed. Then one night I had a dream. In the dream Grandma Ellis was talking to me. We were back in our old house and she was standing in the kitchen baking cookies, she looked just like she did when she was alive. In the dream, she told me that God would supply all my needs, then she told me to go to the store and buy her a newspaper. I walked to the corner store and searched for the Columbus Dispatch, but they did not have any.

I remember arguing with the sales clerk telling him that I had to take my grandmother a paper, so he handed me a paper called The Thrifty Nickel, and said take this to her.

I ran back to the house with the paper, but when I got there, she was gone. I kept yelling her name, but she never answered. I woke up from the dream feeling very confused.

I did not think about the dream anymore until the day I walked into Krogers and just happened to glance at the newspaper stand. There big as day were free editions of the Thrifty Nickel. I picked up one and put it in the cart. Later that night I started looking in the paper at the homes section. I saw a big ad for a section eight house that was for rent. They wanted eight hundred a month. I figured I did not have anything to lose, so the next morning I called the number in the paper and set up an appointment to see the house later that afternoon.

A few weeks earlier, I had written out a list of things that I wanted my house to have. I wanted a fenced yard because I wanted Kacess'ion to be able to play outside without having to worry about her running in the street. I wanted air conditioning, Jessica told me that the summers in Atlanta were always very hot and muggy. I also wanted a dishwasher. I hated washing dishes by hand. I guess my stepmother must have mentally scarred me for life. She made me wash the dishes every day. If she found one dish that did not look clean, she would pull out all the dishes in the cabinet and make me wash them all over again, even the clean ones. My other desire was for a nice, quiet neighborhood. I wanted my daughter and me to feel safe.

I arrived at the house before the owner got there. I was very impressed with the neighborhood. All the lawns were nice, neat, and freshly cut. All of the houses on the block looked well maintained. When I told Jessica the address, she told me that the house was in a very good area.

The house was a cute ranch style home. It was creamed colored with brown trimming and a long brown wrap around porch. The front yard was completely fenced in.

On the right side of the house was a small driveway with a carport. I got out of the car and put Kacess'ion in my baby packsack that hung off my shoulders. The sack hung in front and kept Kacess'ion close to me, but allowed my hands to be free. Jessica had given it to me at my baby shower. I walked around to the back of the house. I could tell from the outside vent that the house had central air conditioning. There was a large apple tree in the back yard. As I walked back around the house, the owner pulled up into the drive way. Something about him looked familiar; it was as if I had seen him somewhere before. He was a short black man with a big stomach and a baldhead. He appeared to be in his late fifty's or early sixties. After staring at him for a while, I realized that he looked like the man from my dream, the sales clerk who had given me the thrifty nickel.

"Hello, I am sorry that I am late. The traffic up I-20 is murder at this time of day. I think it's because of all the construction going on." He said as he held out his hand toward me. "You are Mrs. King?" He asked.

"Yes, "I replied as I shook his hand.

"My name is Mr. Payne."

"It's nice to meet you, Mr. Payne." I said smiling.

"So what do you think of the outside of the house? I just had new siding put up about a year ago."

"It looks nice." I said smiling.

"I see there is an apple tree in the backyard. Can the apples be eaten?"

"Sure can my wife use to make apples pies all the time before she died. We lived in this house for twenty years. After my wife died, I just could not live here anymore. I also could not bring myself to sell it. So I decided to rent it."

"I'm sorry to hear about your wife"

"Yea, she passed away four years ago. She was in a car accident, a drunk driver hit her." I could see the sadness in his eyes.

"Is that the only child that you have?" He asked pointing toward Kacess'ion.

She had started moving around, trying to find a comfortable space on my breast.

Kacess'ion was such a good baby, she hardly ever cried.

"Yes, she is my only one."

"Well follow me and I will show you around the inside of the house." We walked to the front screen door. Most of the homes that I had seen did not have any screen doors, or any screens in the windows,

I was very impressed. After he unlocked the door we walked into the living room. The living room had a fireplace in the corner with a large mirror hanging over it. It was a nice size living room.

"I just had all the walls painted last week, so watch your step. The carpet is only six months old, once I decided that I was going to rent it out, I started making a lot of updates to it. If you decide that you like it, you will be the first tenant." He stated as he guided me to the kitchen.

"All the appliances are new, I decided to keep the ones that me and my wife bought, so if anything goes wrong with the refrigerator or the stove let me know, they are still under warranty."

"Does it have a dishwasher?"

"Yes ma'am, my wife insisted on having one put in when we first moved to the house. The original one gave out about a year before she died so we had to buy a new one. The one in there is five years old but it has not been used in the last four years."

He took me to the master bedroom, it was so nice, it had a big window that faced the large apple tree in the back yard. It also had its own bathroom and a walk in closet. I was very impressed. Then he showed me a second room that was small enough to be an office.

"The house was originally set up to be a one bedroom with a study. My wife and I never had any children, so we never needed more than a one bedroom. When I lived here I turned this room into my office but it can also be used for a second bedroom.

There is a small closet space to store your baby's clothes and toys." He stated, pointing to the door near the window.

"Does the air conditioning work in this house?" I asked.

"Yes ma'am it sure does, just had it serviced last summer. We had a basement put in when we first bought the house. About eight years ago, we transformed the basement into a family room." He stated as he guided me towards a door next to the bathroom in the hallway. I was completely surprised at how nice the house was. The finished basement had a utility room with washer and dryer hookups.

"There is a laundry shoot in the master bedroom that leads down to the basement.

So if you do not feel like walking the laundry down the steps, just throw it down the shoot" He said pointing to a small cabinet door next to the washer faucets. The basement had carpet and cable TV outlets.

"So how many applicants do you have so far?" I knew that anyone who saw this house would want it.

"None, you are the first. I just put the ad in this weekend. Yesterday was the first day that my ad ran." When he said that I knew that this was my house.

"You're asking a fair price for the house." I stated.

"It has been appraised at eighty thousand. When my wife and I bought it, we only paid thirty thousand for it. We put a lot of work into this house over the years. It was my pet project. I own another house about forty-five minutes from here. It is a much bigger house, more rooms, but this house is my favorite. I just could not bring myself to live in it once my wife died. This house has too many memories." He said with a sad look on his face. I felt so bad for him. I knew how it felt to lose someone that you love. I was still trying to get over Linda's murder.

"How much is the deposit?" I asked.

"Same as the rent, eight hundred," he stated.

"I will take it." I replied. I pulled out my checkbook and wrote Mr. Payne a check. Mrs. Francis made sure that each of us opened a checking account. She said it did not matter if we were on welfare. It was important to learn to save money even if it was only ten dollars a month.

"I will need to go to my car and get the application. If everything checks out and the section eight department will approve it, then the house will be yours. If anything goes wrong, I will refund the entire eight hundred dollars."

"That sounds good to me." I replied. We walked out of the house and back to our cars. He handed me the application and I handed him a check.

"I will have it back to you in the morning." I stated as I glanced at it.

"Okay, soon as I get it back from you, I will perform my background checks, if everything checks out, I will give you the paperwork that you need to turn in to section eight." He said smiling.

"Thank you, it was nice meeting you Mr. Payne." I said with a smile

"The pleasure was all mines," he replied as he got into his car. I watched him as he drove away. Then I glanced back at the house.

"Thank you Grandma Ellis." I said aloud. I put Kacess'ion back in her car seat and got back into the car.

Three weeks after I met with Mr. Payne about the house, I moved in. The Love House helped me to get a lot of used furniture from the Furniture bank. I was very grateful to Mrs. Francis. After paying the deposit on the house, and getting my utilities on, I only had seven hundred dollars left of the money my uncle had given me. I wanted to save the rest for emergencies. There was no way I was going to call my uncle and ask for more money.

Jessica and Rita had also received their section eight vouchers. They both found houses that were only thirty minutes away from me. Rita signed up with the state to do title- twenty childcare in her home. Just as I promised, Kacess'ion was her first daycare child. Monica was still waiting on her section eight appointment.

We knew that Monica felt depressed because she was the only one still left in the house.

She had all new roommates and she was not getting along with any of them. So we made sure that she spent a lot of time at our houses. We had card parties, and outings with the kids every weekend. It was very important to the four of us that we remain close friends. We had been through a lot together. Every Sunday, Jessica would cook a big dinner and we would all go over to her house after church. I was truly starting to enjoy my new life in Georgia.

I decided I wanted to start school fall semester, I went down to Georgia State University and signed up for class. Instead of trying to get my associates degree in nursing, I would go for a bachelor's degree. I knew that going to college for four years meant that I would have to stay on welfare, but it was worth the sacrifice.

It was time to get my life back on track. Besides, between grants, student loans and welfare, I could make it; I was determined to make it.

NEW LOVE

PART IV

Love is such a wonderful feeling,

The power of love can cause so much healing.

Love is such a beautiful thing,

God's love is what makes the flowers bloom and the birds sing.

The love that you and I share is unique,

It is not something people find every day of the week.

Meeting you was destiny,

I know that our love was meant to be.

I was made for you and you were made for me.

CHAPTER 14

JUNE 8, 1989

Today was one of the happiest days of my life. Today was graduation day. After four and a half years of struggling through school and raising my daughter, I was finally graduating from Georgia State University. Once I passed my state boards I could work anywhere in the world. The United States was starting to experience a nursing shortage; some hospitals were paying three thousand-dollar sign on bonuses.

"Kacess'ion!" I yelled out the front door.

"Yes Mommy?" Kacess'ion answered running up the sidewalk.

"Come on honey, you have to get dressed. You know that today is mommies big day." I said as I held the screen door open.

"Can I wear the pretty dress that Aunt Monica bought me?" Kacess'ion asked as she walked through the door. Kacess'ion was starting to look more and more like her father every day. She had the same hazel colored eyes, jet black naturally curly hair, and smooth caramel colored skin complexion. I think the only thing she got from me were the dimples and the smile. She had a beautiful smile just like my mother. There was no doubt that Kacess'ion was going to grow up to be a beautiful woman one day. The best thing about Kacess'ion was that her personality matched her looks. She was always respectful to her elders. She was a good child; I hardly ever had to punish her.

She had just had her 5th birthday, Rita, Monica, and Jessica bought her lots of gifts, sometimes I felt like my friends spoiled her too much.

After Kacess'ion and I got dressed, we jumped in my Buick and drove to Jessica's house. It was a beautiful warm day in Atlanta, the warm Georgia air blew my hair as I raced down the highway. I was so excited, and relieved, the last few weeks of school seemed the hardest. I guess it was because I knew I was about to graduate. I glanced over at my daughter. She was singing to the latest sounds of Whitney Houston. She actually had a very pretty voice for a five-year-old. I made a mental note to sign her up for singing lessons. I smiled to my self at the thought of my daughter growing up to be a famous singer.

We slowly pulled into Jessica's long driveway. Jessica had accomplished a lot in the last five years. Jessica had landed a job with one of the largest law firms in Atlanta as a legal secretary and fell in love with one of the lawyers at the firm. She and her husband were married two years ago. She also had a new addition to the family. A cute two-year-old little girl named Jasmine. Jessica no longer lived in the ghetto. She now had a beautiful home in Alpharetta, Georgia.

Kacess'ion and I got out of the car, walked the short distance to her porch, and knocked on the front door. Jessica's oldest son Tom answered the door. Tom had sprouted up to be a very tall, muscular, and handsome young man. Many times Jessica would call me complaining about the latest teenage girl who was trying to snag her son.

"Hi Ms. Karen, Mom is in her room getting dressed. She told me to tell you to go upstairs when you got here."

"Okay." I replied as Kacess'ion and I walked through the door. Jessica and her husband had a very beautiful home. Sometimes I secretly envied Jessica. She was so happy, she was married to a man who adored her, had a good job, and lived in one of the nicest houses on the block.

"Kacess'ion, go outside and play with little Jasmine while mommy talks to Aunt Jessica."

"Okay mommy," she replied as she ran off toward the back yard.

"Jessica!" I yelled up the stairs.

"Hey Karen, come on up." I started walking up the long winding staircase to her bedroom.

"I just came to drop Kacess'ion off. Everyone has to be at the school for our last minute rehearsal. Don't forget it starts at 7:00 p.m."

"Don't worry honey. I would not miss this for the world." Jessica said as she emerged from her walk-in closet. "Where did you say the reception was going to be held?" She asked as she walked toward me putting on her earrings.

"It will be at the Hyatt on Peachtree Street. The reception starts at 9:00 p.m.

Tell Tammy I said thanks for watching Kacess'ion for me."

"No problem." Jessica said smiling.

I left Jessica's house and drove to the university. Everyone was sitting in the auditorium when I arrived. I had my graduation gown in the car; I did not want to risk getting it dirty before tonight. I sat down next to Lisa, one of my fellow classmates.

"Hey girl, what's up?" Lisa asked as I sat down. She was already dressed in her white graduation gown.

"Nothing much, I am just glad that we all finally made it."

"Yea, I know what you mean. When are you planning on taking your boards?"

"I plan to take my boards as soon as I can." I smirked.

"Yea me too, you know it's supposed to be computerized this year."

"I don't care as long as the test has multiple choices." I glanced at my watch.

Rehearsals were supposed to start at 6:00 p.m. I still had fifteen minutes, I watched as some of our other classmates rushed in.

"Mrs. Johnson said that since it's all computerized, we should have our results within three weeks of taking the test, if we pass, our license will be accompanying the results." She stated.

"Wow, that's cool, well I am hoping to be able to take my test within the next two weeks." I replied.

"Have you decided where you want to work? Lisa asked as she moved the tassel on her hat to the other side.

"Yes Grady Hospital, I am going to apply for the internship they have for new grads, they are paying a three thousand dollar sign on bonus." I replied.

"Wow, they must really need nurses bad to be offering that much money. I might go and put in an application there to. How much are they paying hourly?"

"I'm not sure, but anything is better than what I am getting right now, which is nothing." I broke out into a deep laugh.

"Yea I know what you mean." Lisa giggled.

"I heard that Jacky is not going to graduate with us, she flunked her final." Lisa said as she applied lip-gloss to her thin lips.

"Really, that's too bad. I just thank God that I passed, I have been a nervous wreck for the last three weeks. Are you going to the reception tonight?" I asked. Lisa and I had been study partners through most of our college years. She was one of the smartest people I ever met.

"Girl, you know I am. I would not miss it for the world."

A few minutes later, our instructors entered the auditorium and we began rehearsals.

After it was finished, I went to the women's locker room and changed into my graduation gown. I fixed my hair and put on my graduation hat. I looked in the mirror and began putting on my makeup. I felt a sudden wave of sadness overcome me as I thought about Linda. We always talked about how we would feel when we finally graduated. I thought about her often, the police still had not found her killer, her ex-boyfriend had an alibi; they no longer considered him a suspect. The police said that it may have been a random act of violence and because they did not have any witness's, it's possible that they may never find her killer. Linda was very promiscuous, so there was no telling who she may have been dating at the time of her murder. I use to warn her all the time about being too friendly with all those different guys, but she would just laugh at me and tell me not to worry because she could take care of herself. I missed her so much.

The ceremony seemed to go by quickly. At the end, our graduation class threw our hats up in the air. Jessica took pictures of Lisa and me with our diplomas.

That night Jessica, Rita, Monica and I went to the Hyatt. They must have been holding more than one function because the hotel was packed. As we were walking down the hallway, I was so deep into our conversation that I never saw the man holding the wine glass until I ran into him.

"I am so sorry sir." I said as I tried to wipe the wine off his expensive jacket with the napkin I was holding. I was so embarrassed. He was a tall, dark skin, muscular man with a baldhead. I always thought that baldheaded men were so sexy. He looked like he was in his late thirty's. He had a salt and pepper mustache and a well-groomed beard.

He was so fine. He looked like he had just stepped out of a GQ magazine.

"That's okay; I hope that I did not mess up your beautiful dress," he replied with the sexiest, deepest voice I had ever heard.

"No, I think most of the wine got on you." I felt myself blushing.

"Excuse me sir." I said as I started walking back toward my friends.

"Wow. He was too fine." Jessica said as we all walked away.

"Looks like he thought Karen was fine too, he is still looking at her." Rita said as she glanced behind us.

"Hell, he could spill anything he wants to on me," Monica said laughing.

"You guys are silly; I am going into the ladies' room." I said walking toward the women's restroom.

"I need to go to the bathroom too, hey why don't you two go find us a good table." Jessica stated as she followed me into the bathroom. I walked over to the sink and grabbed a paper towel, trying to wipe some of the wine off my dress.

"Hey, didn't you think he was cute?" Jessica asked as she walked into one of the bathroom stalls.

"He was okay." I replied nonchalantly. A few minutes later Jessica emerged from the stall, walked over to the sink, and began washing her hands.

"Karen, you have not had one date in all the time I have known you, aren't you ready to start dating again?" Jessica asked as she looked in the mirror and reapplied her lipstick.

"No, I don't want to date anyone. I am happy with my life the way it is.

Kacess'ion keeps me very occupied." I said as I reapplied my face powder.

"Yea, but Kacess'ion cannot provide sexual healing. Don't you ever get horny?"

Jessica was always hounding me about dating. She even tried to set me up on blind dates with her husband's friends, but I always declined the offers.

"No, I don't really think about sex. It was never that enjoyable to me anyway." I answered as I smoothed down my hair. Jessica turned and looked at me. I could see the concern in her eyes.

"Karen, you can't let what Clyde did to you stop you from having a loving relationship with a man. Not all men are the same."

"I'm fine just as I am Jessica, come on lets go find Rita and Monica." I said as I walked out of the bathroom. I was not in the mood to hear Jessica lecture me about my love life. I did not need or want a man. I was happy being single.

Monica and Rita had found a nice table in the middle of the room. A lot of people were dancing as the DJ played the latest R&B tunes.

"Excuse me ma'am, but would you like to dance?" The deep voice behind me sounded familiar. I turned around in my seat to see who was tapping me on the shoulder.

To my surprise, it was the handsome man I had spilled the drink on earlier that evening.

"No thank you, but thanks for the offer." I said politely.

"Well do you mind if I sit here for a moment?" He asked pointing to the empty chair beside me. I really did not want him to sit down, but Jessica answered before I could reply.

"Sure, sit down, no one is sitting there," she said smiling. I turned toward her and gave her an evil look. She acted as if she did not see me looking at her and just kept smiling at the handsome stranger.

"Allow me to formally introduce myself, my name is David Smith," he replied offering me his hand.

"Well it's nice to meet you Mr. Smith. My name is Karen King." I shook his hand and then quickly put my hand back in my lap.

"Did you know someone who graduated from Georgia State?" He asked.

"Yes, I graduated." I laughed.

"Oh, well congratulations. What was your major?" It was obvious that he was making him self rather comfortable. He had the sexiest smile and the prettiest white teeth.

"Nursing" I replied.

"Well isn't that nice. I am in the medical profession also," he said smiling.

"What do you do?" Monica asked, obviously butting into our conversation.

"I am a doctor; I deliver babies for a living." He laughed.

"Wow, that's really impressive." Rita said taking a sip of her margarita, and sneaking a peek at me.

"Hey Monica, you said that you wanted to dance, why don't the two of you hit the dance floor." I said glancing to where all the couples were dancing. I was ready for him to leave. He was making me nervous.

"Sure, you want to dance?" Monica asked. David gave me a bewildered look.

"Sure,"He said as he stood up and led Monica to the dance floor.

"Girl, what's wrong with you? The man is obviously interested in you," Jessica said frowning.

"Well I am not interested in him or any other man for that matter, so you can stop trying to play matchmaker. I will be right back, I am going to go and call Kacess'ion.

You know how she acts when she starts getting sleepy." I stood up and walked toward the area where I had seen the payphones. After calling Kacess'ion and listening to her, tell me how much fun she was having, I purposely took my time getting back to the table.

"Girl, what took you so long? All that man did the whole time we were dancing was kept asking me questions about you. He waited fifteen minutes before he left."

It was obvious from Monica's tone of voice that she was irritated with me.

"I know it didn't take that damn long to make a phone call." Jessica stated sipping on her drink and cutting her eyes at me.

"Will you guys get off my case please?" I said in an agitated voice. They were starting to get on my nerves.

"He said he had to rush to the hospital, one of his mothers was in labor and he was on call tonight. He was here because his niece graduated. He asked me to give this to you." Monica said as she handed me a white business card.

"He said he owns a practice that he shares with two other doctors," Rita stated smiling at me. I looked at the business card and then put it in my purse.

"Thanks for the information." I said sarcastically. They all sighed and gave me a look like I was a lost cause.

We stayed for another two hours then I drove home. Kacess'ion spent the night over Jessica's house. When I entered my home, I went into the kitchen and kicked my shoes off, the heels had started making my feet hurt. I poured myself a glass of orange juice and then sat down at the table. I started thinking about the handsome doctor. I reached and pulled his business card out of my purse. It had his office, home, and cell phone number on it.

"There is no way I am calling this man," I said aloud as I ripped up the card and threw it in the trash. My life was peaceful right now and that is how I wanted it to stay. I had already had one bad experience with a man; I was determined not to go through it again. Clyde had me fooled; I thought he was so fine and so nice when I first met him. After we were married he turned into a monster. There was no way I was going to give another man the opportunity to hurt me the way that Clyde had. I turned off all the lights and went to bed.

CHAPTER 15

It had been three weeks since I took the nursing board examination, I had been on edge ever since. Every day I would wait anxiously for the mail carrier to arrive, sometimes even fussing aloud, when he was late. Once I saw the mail carrier pull off, I would rush to the mailbox. When I did not see anything, a flood of disappointment would come over me for a moment, then I would tell myself, relax Karen, maybe tomorrow.

Today was just like all the other days; I sat on the couch and watched the clock. At 2:00 p.m., I started looking for the mail carrier. I walked to the window and peeked outside. To my surprise, the mail carrier was pulling out of my driveway. I waited for him to pull off, and then I opened the screen door and checked the mailbox. I flipped through the mail until I found the letter from the nursing board. I threw all the other letters on the floor and rushed to the telephone and dialed Monica's number.

"Hello?" Monica answered.

"It came!" I shouted without saying hello.

"Well did you pass?" I could hear the excitement in her voice.

"I don't know, I haven't opened it yet."

"Karen, open the letter," she demanded.

"Oh Monica, what if I failed. I worked so hard over the last four and a half years, I studied for two weeks before I took the test. What if I didn't study enough?" I whined.

I could feel the butterflies in my stomach. My hands were starting to sweat.

"Karen, open the damn letter before you give us both a heart attack!" Monica yelled.

"Okay, okay, here it goes." I tore the envelope open. As I was unfolding the results, something fell on the floor. When I reached down to pick it up, I realized that it was my nursing license.

"Monica, I passed!" I yelled and started jumping up and down like I had just won the lottery. Kacess'ion came running into the kitchen.

"Mommy, are you okay?" She asked. I realized that I had scared her.

"Yes baby. Mommy is okay. I am just excited because I passed my test." I was so happy. I had been waiting on this day for a very long time.

"Monica, I will call you back."

"Okay, congratulations. You know that we are all going to have to get together and celebrate. I'll talk to you later." Then she hung up.

I was so happy I picked Kacess'ion up, twirled her around in the air, and then started dancing around the room with her in my arms as if she was light as a feather.

"Your mommy did it." I said as I hugged her and then put her back down on the floor. I picked up the telephone and dialed Rita's number.

"Hello?" Rita answered. I could hear her daycare children in the background.

"I did it Rita. I passed my boards. I received my license in the mail this afternoon." I said staring at the test results.

"Congratulations, I am so happy for you."

"After four and a half long years, I am finally going to reach my dream of being an obstetrics and neonatal nurse. Now I can start applying for jobs."

"Cool, have you called anyone else yet?" She asked.

"Yea, I told Monica. I have not talked to Jessica yet. I am going to call her right now, hold on while I click over." I clicked over to my three-way line and called Jessica's work number.

"Hello, this is Raymond & Johnson Associates." Jessica answered in a very professional voice.

"Jessica, it's me Karen; hold on Rita is on the other line," I clicked so that I could talk to both of them at the same time.

"I passed my exams Jessica. I received my license today."

"Congratulations Karen, when are we all going to get together and celebrate?"

"Let's do it this weekend," Rita suggested.

"That sounds good to me," I replied.

"Hey Karen, did you ever call that doctor?" Jessica asked switching the subject.

"I told you that I am not interested in dating anyone." I loved my friends but sometimes they could be annoying.

"What are you so afraid of?" Rita asked.

"I'm not afraid of anything, I am just not interested."

"You are going to grow old and lonely if you don't start dating," Jessica said in a sarcastic voice. I was not in the mood to talk about my love life, or lack there of.

"Well, I have to go. I have to take Kacess'ion to her dance class. I will talk to you guys this weekend," I quickly hung up the phone. I sat down on the couch and stared at my license.

"Thank you God. You have brought me a very long way," I said aloud.

The next morning I dropped Kacess'ion off at school and started putting in applications. My first stop was Grady Hospital; I walked into the human resources department and filled out an application for the OB internship. After applying at three other places I treated myself to lunch. Within two days, Grady hospital called me to schedule an interview. I went to the thrift store and bought two nice looking business suites, I wanted to look as professional as possible. I even went to the beauty salon the day before my interview and had my hair done and my nails neatly manicured.

The next morning I was sitting in the lobby of Grady hospital, when the interviewer called my name.

"Ms. King?" I looked up.

"Yes, I am Ms. King," I stated as I stood up. She walked over to me and shook my hand.

"Hello, my name is Mrs. Price. Thank you for coming, please follow me," she said as she turned and started walking back to her office. She was a slender, attractive, middle age Caucasian woman, with long sandy brown hair and long legs. I followed her into her office.

"Please take a sit," she said pointing to the chairs in front of her desk. She closed her office door, walked around her desk, and sat down.

"So, you would like to begin our internship program?"

"Yes." I replied.

"Can I see your R.N. license, social security card, and CPR card? I will also need a recent physical and TB results." I handed her all of my paper work. I felt so nervous; I could feel my palms starting to sweat. I was determined that I was going to make it through this interview. She began asking me questions about nursing, my education, work experience, and my reasons for wanting to work at Grady Hospital. After the interview, she took me on a tour of the OB ward. As we were walking past the nurse's station I glanced to my right and looked right into David Smith's face. He smiled and walked over to my interviewer.

"Hello Mrs. Price," the interviewer immediately started blushing.

"Hello Dr. Smith, how are you doing today?" She asked smiling.

"Fine, thank you," he turned toward me.

"Hello Karen," I could not believe he still remembered my name. He extended his hand toward me. I gently shook his hand.

"Hello Sir." I replied.

"Oh please, don't call me sir; the two of you have a good day," David said smiling. He took one last glance at me then turned and walked away.

"You know Dr. Smith?" Mrs. Price asked with a surprised look on her face.

I figured telling her yes might help me to get the job so I said yes. After she finished giving me a tour of the rest of the unit, she thanked me for my time. I went to three more interviews that week, all of them sounded promising but Grady hospital was the only one offering the OB internship.

I was in a deep sleep the next morning when the telephone rang. I reached over to my nightstand and picked up the phone.

"Hello." I answered trying to clear my throat.

"Hello Ms. King, this is Mrs. Price from Grady Hospital," the woman on the other end said cheerfully. I quickly sat straight up in bed.

"Hello Mrs. Price, how are you doing?"

"Oh I am doing just fine, thank you, I am calling to offer you a position in our new grad OB internship. Are you interested?" She asked.

"Oh yes, I'm very interested," I replied. My heart started beating fast.

"Good, you will need to come in and fill out the necessary paperwork. During the internship, you will be paid twelve dollars an hour. After the internship is completed, and if you pass, the final exam and your clinical, you will be employed in a full time position on our seven to three shift making nineteen dollars an hour plus benefits and plus your sign on bonus."

"Okay," I said smiling I was so excited the most money I had ever made was eight dollars an hour, as a clerk at the Columbus Police Department.

"Please come to the hospital Monday morning at nine o'clock to complete the employee package and orientation," Mrs. Price said in a cheerful voice.

"Thank you Mrs. Price," I said as I stood up.

"Your welcome, have a nice day," she replied, and then she hung up the phone.

"I want to thank you lord, for all your wonderful blessings!" I shouted aloud. I thought back to the day when I was in my living room in Columbus, praying to God that he would make a way for me. I picked up the phone and called Monica at work.

Monica had taken out a small business loan a year ago and opened up an African American bookstore. She also sold her books online; her business was really doing well. I dialed the number to her store.

"Ebony Books, may I help you." The young clerk answered in a chipper voice.

"May I speak with Ms. Lopez?" I asked.

"One moment please," the clerk put me on hold. I held the phone to my ear and walked over to my closet so that I could figure out what I was going to wear today.

"Hello, this is Ms. Lopez," she answered. Monica still had a strong Puerto Rican accent.

"Hey, what's up, it's Karen." I said as I began searching through the clothes in my closet.

"Hey, what's up Karen?" She said in a cheerful voice.

"The lady from Grady called me this morning; I have been accepted for the internship."

"Congratulations, hey did you ever call the handsome doctor?" Monica asked.

"No Monica I did not call him, but guess where I saw him?" I asked as I threw the clothes that I had chosen onto my bed.

"Where?" She asked.

"At Grady, he must have been delivering a baby; I guess he sends all of his patients there."

"Did he see you?" Monica asked.

"Yes, we spoke."

"So why didn't you call him, you are letting a good man get away." I could hear the disappointment in her voice.

"Monica, I am just not ready to start dating anyone. I guess I am still dealing with the things that happened in my marriage. I am scared of getting hurt again. I do not ever want to go through another relationship like that. I guess the easiest way to keep from getting hurt is to stay away from men." For some reason I felt the need to confide in her.

"Karen it's been more than five years since you were with Clyde. It's time to move on." Monica had not wasted anytime reentering the dating scene once she left The Love House. In the last four years, she had been in at least three relationships. The latest man that she was dating was the vice president of a bank in downtown Atlanta.

"I guess I am just not like you Monica. It's more difficult for me," I sighed.

"Listen, I have some customers waiting on me out front. How about we meet for lunch sometime this week?"

"Yea, that would be nice, well I will talk to you later," I replied. After I got off the phone I got myself dressed, then I woke Kacess'ion up and helped her to get ready for school. I decided that tonight, I was going to celebrate with my daughter. I planned to take her out for ice cream and a movie.

That evening, after Kacess'ion and I came back from our outing, I gave her a bath, read her a bedtime story and tucked her in the bed. I was in my finished basement watching television when the telephone rang.

"Hello?" I answered.

"Hello Karen," at first I did not recognize the deep voice on the other end of the phone.

"May I ask who is calling?" I asked, with a raised eyebrow.

"It's David Smith."

"Mr. Smith, how did you get my phone number?" I asked with surprise. As soon as I said the words, Monica's face popped in my head. She had better not have given him my number.

"I have a lot of connections at Grady Hospital. Some of my connections owe me favors," he said with a chuckle. I could not believe he was able to get my number from human resources. I thought that type of information was supposed to be confidential.

"Listen, I really didn't get to talk to you the first time we met. I wanted to know if you would go out to dinner with me." Hearing his sexy voice sent chills down my spine.

"Mr. Smith, I don't know who you bribed to get my number, but I am not interested in going out with you or anyone else for that matter."

"Are you married or have a boyfriend?" He asked.

"If you must know, I am legally separated from my husband, and no I do not have a boyfriend. Mr. Smith, you are a very handsome man who could have any woman at Grady Hospital. Ask someone else." Then I promptly hung up the phone. The nerve of that man, I guess he was use to having women eat out of his hands. He was obviously not use to women turning him down. I refused to let another man sweet talk his way into my life the way Clyde did.

Monday morning I dropped Kacess'ion off at school and went to my orientation. There were about twenty other people in the class. As I entered the room, I heard someone call my name. I searched the room to see who was calling me. Then I saw Lisa, my friend from Georgia State waving her hand at me. I smiled and walked over to her. Lisa was a very attractive heavy set, Caucasian woman with long blond hair, green eyes, and dimples.

"Hey Lisa, so you decided to put in an application," I said sitting down next to her.

"When you told me about the sign on bonus, I decided to check it out. Besides OB was my favorite rotation in school," Lisa replied as she opened her orientation package and started reading it. During orientation, the instructor explained the qualifications necessary to complete the internship and obtain a full time job. We would have to be available for all three shifts during the internship. The orientation lasted for four hours. As I walked out of Grady Hospital, I began smiling to myself. I was finally on my way.

CHAPTER 16

During the first week in class we went over a lot of rules and regulations, and watched films on safety, and universal precautions. I was already familiar with all the films. In nursing school our teachers had stressed the importance of hand washing, wearing gloves, and not recapping used needles. Health care workers were starting to contact HIV and Hepatitis from contaminated blood and accidental needle sticks. After each film, we had to take a mini quiz to make sure that we were paying attention. I received a 95% on each one of my quizzes. We also went over a lot of the paper work that the nurses and doctors used. We had to go over documentation, flow sheets, assessment sheets, IV therapy procedures, and Automatic IV Pumps. I did not feel very confident about starting IV's. I always seemed to have a hard time locating the vein.

On one particular day, I needed three successful sticks to pass that portion of the clinical. I was so nervous. I had stuck five people and had only gotten two successful sticks. The day was almost over and I was starting to panic. Another R.N. who worked full time at Grady came to the rescue and saved my day.

"How many more sticks does she need Mrs. Adams?" The young male nurse asked my teacher.

"She needs three and she only has two. There are not going to be any more patients coming through for surgery until this afternoon. I am afraid she is not going to pass this portion of her clinical," Mrs. Adams said with a concerned look on her face. Mrs. Adams was a very nice teacher. She always went out of her way for the students, even to the point of being easy on us when it came to grading. I knew that she was not going to be able to bend the rules this time.

"She can start an IV on me, I don't mind," he said with a smile.

"You are going to let her stick you?" Another nurse asked with a look of disbelief.

"Sure, needles don't bother me, hell I like a little pain," he laughed. I looked at my teacher to see what she was going to say.

"Well, the rules don't say the needle sticks have to come from a patient. So if you are willing to let her stick you then I will allow it."

"Thank you so much," I said to the male nurse.

"No problem," he grabbed an overhead table and a chair and sat down. I went over to the nurse's station and got all the supplies I needed to start the IV. I placed everything on the table, and then applied the tourniquet to his upper arm.

"Make sure that you have the tourniquet on tight. This will help to stabilize the vein." I followed his instruction, and then started searching for a good vein to use. It was easy to locate the blue vein on him because of his light complexion. I prepped the area with an alcohol pad and then prepared my needle for entry.

"Watch your angle," he said as he guided my hand. I inserted the needle, and then looked for the flashback that would let me know that I had entered the vein. To my delight, blood started filling the little window on the needle. I continued with the rest of the procedure and successfully started the IV. I was so happy. Everyone in the surgery department that was watching us started applauding when I stated that I was finished.

The next week we were each assigned a R.N. to follow and assist. My assignment was to follow a black nurse named Roberta. She told me that she had been a RN for eight years and had worked in OB for six of those years. We had three patients who were in labor. I followed her from room to room, doing whatever she instructed me to do. One of our patients was a seventeen-year-old girl named Stacy. This was her first baby and she had been in labor for ten hours.

"I want you to go in and check her vital signs," Roberta said as she handed me an automatic blood pressure cuff. I knocked on the door then entered the room. Her mother was standing next to her bed holding her hand as she coaxed her through a labor pain.

"Mommy, it hurts so badly," she cried.

"I know honey, just try to relax," her mother said as she wiped the sweat off her daughter's forehead with a washcloth.

"Hello, my name is Karen; I am assisting your daughter's nurse. I just need to check her vitals signs." I said to the mother as I walked to the other side of the bed.

"Hello Stacy, I need to check your vitals signs, how fast are your contractions coming?" I asked.

"They are coming about every five minutes," her mother answered.

"Okay, I am going to go ahead and take your blood pressure before your next contraction hits." I informed Stacy as I applied the cuff to her arm. After I took the vitals and recorded them, I stood by the bed and rubbed her back as another contraction hit her. There was a knock at the door.

"Hello Stacy, it's me, I need to check and see how far you have dilated," Roberta stated as she walked into the room and put on examination gloves.

"Okay." Stacy said meekly. I walked to the end of the bed near Roberta. I did not want to miss anything. Roberta opened her legs and gently inserted her fingers into Stacy's vagina.

"Well, it looks like you are going to witness your first birth, Karen. Stacy has dilated ten centimeters." I walked back to the head of the bed and gently pushed back hair from Stacy's sweat soaked forehead.

"It will not be much longer sweetheart," I said softly.

"Good, I can't take too much more of this," Stacy said weakly.

"Karen, go to the nurses station and page Dr. Smith. Let him know that Miss Cox is ready to deliver. His number is up on the board above the phone." I could not believe my ears. David was Stacy's doctor. I walked out of the room and over to the nurse's station. I dialed David's pager number and then waited for him to call back. About five minutes later the phone rang.

"Hello, this is Dr. Smith," My heart felt like it skipped a beat. There was something so sexy about his voice.

"Hello Dr. Smith, this is Ms. King, your patient Stacy Cox has dilated to 10cm.

There was a pause on the other end of the phone. For a minute, I thought maybe he did not hear me.

"Okay Karen, I will be there, I am in the lounge area." I hung up the phone without saying goodbye. I walked back to Stacy's room. Roberta had already started setting up the equipment that Dr. Smith would need.

"Karen, I need to run and check on another patient. If I am not back by the time the doctor gets here, just hand him whatever he asks you for."

"Okay," I stated as I washed my hands and put on gloves and a hospital surgery gown. A few minutes after she left the room, there was another knock on the door. David entered the room.

"Hello Miss Cox. I hear that you are ready," he said as he washed his hands and put on his sterile gloves. He walked over to me and I helped him to put on his surgery gown. I could smell the expensive cologne that he had on, he smelled so good.

The neonatal team came in and prepared everything for the baby's arrival. I was so excited. I never witnessed a birth before. In my clinical at the university, it seemed like all the patients had their babies either before I got there or had them after I left. I had a new respect for David. It was obvious that he was a very skilled doctor. He spoke soothing words to Stacy as he guided the baby's head out of the birth canal. When the baby's head finally emerged Stacy let out a loud scream. She had chosen to have her baby natural. A decision that I thought was very brave. Not many women could stand having a baby without receiving any medication.

After David suctioned the baby's nose and mouth, it let out a strong cry. I felt tears come to my eyes. I was present to witness new life entering the world. I had been dreaming for four and a half years about this experience. David finished suctioning the baby, and then he pulled the baby the rest of the way out of the birth canal.

"Congratulations, you have a beautiful granddaughter. Would you like to cut the cord?" He asked Stacy's mother. She started crying.

"Yes," she said sniffing, trying to control her tears. She walked over to the end of the bed, took the scissors from David and snipped the cord. David applied the clamp and then quickly handed the baby to the neonatal staff that was anxiously waiting behind us. As the neonatal staff worked on the baby, David worked quickly to deliver the after birth and stitch up Stacy's perineum area.

"Her apgar score is an eight," the neonatal nurse stated. They wrapped the baby up in a blanket, applied a small cap to her head, and then handed her to her waiting mother's arms.

"She is beautiful," I said trying not to cry.

After David checked on Stacy to make sure she was doing well, he helped me clean up the supplies that we had used for the delivery, and then we exited the room. It surprised me that he was willing to help me. Doctors usually do not help the nurses, or at least that is what all the experienced nurses told me.

"You did a wonderful job in there Karen," he said with a smile.

"You are the one who did all the work," I replied trying not to blush.

"That's my last patient for a few hours. I do not expect any more deliveries until later tonight; would you like to have lunch with me?" He asked as he walked toward the nurse's desk to get Stacy's chart so that he could do his documentation and write orders.

"Gosh, you have to come back again tonight?" I asked.

"Yes, when I am on call, I am on call for twenty-four hours."

"I appreciate the offer, but I need to leave early, I have to pick my daughter up from school. I am not going to take a lunch today." I knew that I was making up an excuse. All I needed to do was call Rita and she would have picked Kacess'ion up for me.

"Oh, well maybe next time," David replied with a disappointed look. I walked away from the nurse's station and went to find Roberta. I did not trust myself around Dr. Smith. He was just too sexy.

CHAPTER 17

I had been at Grady for four weeks and it was my turn to work the eleven to seven graveyard shifts. I woke up late and had to rush Kacess'ion over to Rita's house. When I entered the parking lot across from Grady Hospital, I quickly turned off the ignition and got out of the car. As I was locking my car door, I felt something sharp slightly poking me in my back.

"Unlock the door and get back into the car," a low male voice said from behind me. I could feel the heat from his breath on my neck. I felt a sickening chill go down my spine. I suddenly felt weak I knew that if I got back into my car, this man was going to rape me or worse murder me. I glanced at the bottle of Mace that was dangling from my key chain. I knew I would have to turn around to my assailant before I could use it. I heard a small still voice in my head say, "Drop the keys." I let the keys fall to the ground.

"Can I pick up my keys? My hands are shaking." I asked in a timid shaky voice.

"Don't try anything funny or I will kill you," he whispered. I kneeled down and grabbed my keys by the maze container, flipped the cap with my thumb, and then I turned around and let out a loud scream as I sprayed the man in his face. He yelled out a curse word, and then I felt a sharp pain in my abdomen.

I grabbed my stomach and screamed in agony. As I fell to the ground, I heard someone yelling from a distance. Then what sounded like two people fighting. I glanced down at the bright red blood that was covering my hand. I started feeling very light headed. Before I lost consciousness, I saw David Smith kneel down beside me with a concerned look on his face.

When I woke up, I realized that I was in a hospital bed. I raised my hand to touch my face. I had a nasogastric tube in my nose and an oxygen mask on my face. I glanced to the left; and saw my heartbeat and pulse on a heart monitor machine. I glanced to my right and saw Monica sitting in a chair reading a book. Monica must have realized that I was moving because she jumped up out of the chair and came over to my bed.

"Karen, you're awake," she said as she pushed the call light so that the nurse would come to my room. I could not talk because I had the tube down my throat. I just looked at her. There was a knock at the door, and then the nurse entered the room.

"Ms Lynch, She is awake," Monica said in an excited voice. The nurse checked my vitals signs. Then she turned to Monica.

"I will be right back, I have to call Dr. Moseley and let him know that she is awake. Then she turned and left the room.

"We thought that we were going to lose your girl. You have had everyone so worried. I could hear what she was saying but I just could not respond. My eyelids grew heavy and I closed my eyes again. When I woke up Dr. Moseley and Nurse Lynch were in my room. My nose and throat felt so sore. I put my hand up to my face and realized that the nasogastric tube and the oxygen mask were gone.

"Well, hello Ms. King," the black doctor said smiling.

"How long have I been here?" I asked weakly.

"You have been in the hospital for three weeks. The knife did major damage to your inside organs and we had to do emergency surgery. You lost a lot of blood we almost lost you. Thank God, that Dr. Smith and Dr. Samuel were in the parking lot when the man attacked you. We will keep you here for another couple of weeks for observation and some therapy." Then Dr. Moseley and Nurse Lynch left the room. At first, I thought I was dreaming, but when I tried to move the pain in my abdomen let me know it was real. Monica entered the room right after they left. She walked to my bedside table and poured a glass of water.

"Are you thirsty?" She asked.

"Yes," I whispered. She reached on the side of my bed and pushed the control to raise the head of my bed. Once she was satisfied that I was high enough to drink, she put the straw to my mouth. I grabbed the straw in between my lips and started sucking. The cool water felt good as it went down my dry and sore throat.

"Where is my daughter?" I whispered after she took the cup away from my mouth.

"Don't worry. She is over Rita's house. She is fine." There was a knock at the door. Ms Lynch reentered the room.

"How are you feeling Karen?" She asked as she walked over to the side of my bed and pulled back the covers so that she could look at the large dressing on my stomach.

"I'm in a lot of pain." I winced and frowned up my face as she pulled the tape away from my skin and began changing the dressing on my abdomen.

"Dr. Moseley ordered you some Vicodin. I will bring you two of them when I am finished changing your dressing. The police will be coming to see you tomorrow so that you can file charges against the man who attacked you. They wanted to come today, but the doctor said you were too weak." After she finished changing my dressing, she left the room.

"The guy who attacked you was wanted in two other states on rape, murder, and car jacking. He was on the run, which is probably why he attacked you. He must have needed to change cars so that the police would not be able to catch him." Monica said as she picked up the remote control and turned on the television.

Scenes from that day flashed quickly through my mind. I remembered seeing Dr. Smith before I blacked out.

"I guess I should be grateful that Dr. Smith was there," I said smiling. I suddenly felt very guilty for the way I had been treating him over the last few months. Now it seemed like I owed him my life.

"That reminds me; he made me promise to call him once you were able to talk again. He has been coming over here to see you every day," she said as she picked up her purse. She pulled out a business card then walked over to the phone and dialed his number. I wanted to object to her calling him, but I was just too weak.

"Hello Dr. Smith this is Monica, I was calling to let you know that Karen is awake, they removed the nasogastric tube and she is talking. I think she is going to be okay. I will see you when you get here," she said into the phone, and then she hung the phone back on the receiver, sat back in her chair, and continued flipping through the channels.

There was another knock on the door and then the nurse entered. She gave me some pain medication then left the room. I was looking at the news when I drifted back to sleep. When I awaked again, David was standing next to the bed holding my hand.

"Hello sleepy," he said with a big grin.

"Hello Dr. Smith," I whispered. My throat was still very sore.

"Please, call me David," I glanced over to where Monica had been sitting and realized that she was not there.

"Where did Monica go?" I asked.

"She was really tired so I told her to go home and get some sleep. I told her I would sit here with you." He pulled the chair that Monica had been sitting in closer to the bed and sat down.

"I owe you my life David, thank you for helping me," I said with a smile.

"I'm just glad that I was there. I had just finished delivering a baby, me and another doctor where on our way to our cars when we heard you scream." He was staring at me as if I was something that he had never seen before. I ran my hand through my hair.

"I know that I must look horrible," I said weakly.

"You look beautiful to me." He replied as he pushed a strand of my hair off my forehead.

"I don't know how I can ever repay you for saving my life."

"I will settle for dinner," he said with a smile.

"I guess I owe you at least that much," I said blushing.

"Karen, I know that this might not be the most appropriate time for what I am about to say." He took a long pause and just stared at me, and then he continued.

"I want you to know that your friend Monica told me about the abuse that your husband put you through. She told me that she met you in a domestic violence shelter in Ohio. Now I understand why you keep turning me down. At first I was starting to think that I had three noses growing on my face," he chuckled.

"What!" My eyes grew wide. I could not believe Monica betrayed me.

"She had no right to tell you my private business!" I said frowning I was going to make sure that I gave her a piece of my mind when I saw her again.

"Maybe she didn't, but I am glad that she did. Karen, I am not going to hurt you. Not all men are the same. I just want the opportunity to get to know you."

"Why? You can have any woman in this hospital, why are you so interested in me?" I asked.

"I really can't explain it. I really do not understand it myself. I guess it must have been love at first sight. The first time I looked into your eyes, I knew I had to make you mine. You are the most beautiful dark skin woman I have ever seen, the sadness in your eyes makes me want to hug you, love you, and protect you. When I realized that man had attacked you I felt like my heart skipped a beat. I would have beaten the guy to a pulp, but I knew I had to get you back to the hospital," David said in a low voice. I could feel his love I knew that he was pouring his heart out to me. Tears started forming in my eyes. "All I am asking you for is a chance to show you that I am not like your husband, or any other man you may have had in your life." David gently ran the palm of his hand over my cheek. His hand felt so soft and warm.

"Well, you did save my life; I guess you can't be too bad." I said smiling. He leaned over and kissed me on the cheek.

"I'll let you get some rest. Oh, I almost forgot, I bought these for you," he pointed to a large bouquet of flowers and a gift basket. He walked over to the table, picked up the gift basket, and brought it over to the table next to my bed. It had lots of fruit, crackers, cheese, and candy in it.

"The doctor will probably have you on a liquid diet for a day or two, and then he will advance you to a soft diet before he puts you back on solid foods. You can eat these when you start eating solid foods again."

"Thank you David," I said looking at the beautiful basket. I wanted to pick it up, but I was feeling too weak.

"I'll be back to check on you later, I am working here tonight. I have a woman that should be having her baby soon."

"Okay, I will see you later." After he walked out the door, I closed my eyes and fell back into a deep sleep.

They kept me in the hospital for an additional two weeks. David came to visit me every day. The night before the hospital discharged me, David surprised me by having food delivered to my room.

"I am off tonight and since you are going home tomorrow, I thought we would celebrate. I figured you would enjoy eating something other than hospital food," he said as he moved the flowers that were on a big round table and put a silk tablecloth on it. He picked up a bag that he had brought in and pulled out two candles and a candleholder.

He had the hospital staff bring in two chairs. Then he helped me out of the bed and led me to a chair. I still felt a little weak, but the therapy had helped me a lot.

"It seems that you are a man full of surprises." I said as I watched him pick up the radio that he had brought in and put in a Sade CD. He finished prepping the table, lit the candles, and then sat down.

"I can't believe that you went through all this for me." I said as I bowed my head to say a quick prayer over the food. After I finished praying, David began fixing my plate. The food smelled delicious. We had roast beef, mashed potatoes smothered in gravy, fresh buttered peas, and honey buttered rolls.

"You haven't seen anything yet. I am a very romantic man, I believe in making my woman feel special." I did not think he realized what he had just said. I wondered if he was labeling me as his woman. During dinner we had a long talk, he told me about his ex-wife and I told him about Kacess'ion, David did not have any children. We had one thing in common; we both had experienced abusive childhoods. He told me that his father had been an alcoholic, and that he had beat him throughout his childhood. When he was sixteen, he ran away from home and moved in with his uncle. His uncle was a doctor, which is how he ended up getting into medicine. We talked late into the night.

The next day Jessica, Rita, Monica, and Kacess'ion came to take me home. Just before we were ready to leave, David showed up and offered to give me a ride.

"You don't have to take me home, my friends will take me." I said as I put on my shoes.

"He can take you home if he wants to, it will save us some gas," Jessica said laughing.

"Yea, let him take you home, Kacess'ion is going to stay with me until you are better. She loves playing with the new kids that I just signed into my daycare," Rita said as she winked at me.

"Are you sure you don't mind?" I asked David. I did not want to intrude on him or make him think I was trying to take advantage of his kindness.

"I would not have offered if it was not something I wanted to do," he said as he helped me to put on my jacket.

"Well, okay, I replied.

"So this is your little girl?" David asked smiling at Kacess'ion.

"Yes, this is my big helper," I said gently rubbing Kacess'ions hair.

"She is a beautiful little girl, just like her mother," he reached into his pocket, pulled out a ten-dollar bill, and handed it to Kacess'ion. "This is for being such a good helper for your mommy." Kacess'ions eyes grew wide as she looked at the money.

"Thank you," she said shyly.

"You are welcome," he replied then he turned toward me. "I am going to go and take this stuff down to the car, I will be right back." He said as he picked up a couple of my bags and the flowers that he had bought me. As soon as he walked out the door, my friends started in on me.

"Girl, you had better not let that man slip away," Jessica said with her hands on her hips.

"Monica, why did you tell him about Clyde?" I said as I gave her my serious look.

"I knew you would probably get upset with me for telling him about Clyde, but I just could not let you mess it up with him. I figured that if he knew about your situation, that he would be patient with you," she said apologetically.

"Well, that was personal, and you had no right to disclose my business." I said frowning and slightly raising my voice.

"I am sorry," Monica said as she continued picking up my things off the bed.

"Well, I am glad she did. Your ass was about to lose a good man. Instead of being upset with her, you should be thanking her," Jessica said in a sarcastic voice as she rolled her eyes at me. I knew she had a good point; I had been treating him pretty badly before my attack. I decided not to dwell on the subject anymore.

My friends helped me to get into David's Lexus. When we arrived at my house, he called his business partner and asked him to cover for him. Then he fixed me dinner and tucked me in. He made a pallet on the floor next to my bed, and we talked until I heard him snoring. I smiled to myself; it was obvious that he was very tired. I had never met a man so sweet. I could feel the ice barricade that I had been wearing for the last five and a half years beginning to melt. For the first time in years, I was falling in love . . .

CHAPTER 18

After two weeks of recovering at home, I was ready to return to Grady to complete the last three weeks of my internship. Everyone at the hospital heard about what happened to me. People I did not even know were coming up to me and asking me how I was doing. They told me that the incident had been on the news for a whole week. Lisa walked up to me on my way to class.

"Hey girl, are you all right?"

"Yes I am fine, thank you," I replied as I shuffled the papers in my hand.

"We heard that the guy was wanted in Detroit and in Ohio, I am glad he is in jail." She stated.

"Yea, I know I was told that the guy had killed a woman in Ohio and had raped and robbed a woman in Detroit," I replied.

"It's a good thing that Dr. Smith was on his way home when it happened."

"I know," I said as I glanced at my watch.

"The hospital has set up security guards in all the parking lots," Lisa said as she ran her fingers through her long hair.

"That's good, I know that they have them in most of the parking lots. I guess that since that one was across the street, they did not think it was necessary. Well I have to go; you know how the teachers hate for us to be late to class." I said as I slowly started taking baby steps away from her.

"Oh by the way, I passed my clinical, I start working OB next week. I heard they are going to start training us for the emergency room, once they are sure that we are comfortable with working OB. I guess the ER must be really busy," she stated with a grin on her face.

"Congratulations," I walked over to her and patted her on the back.

"I pray that I pass my clinical," I said smiling.

"I'm sure that you will," she said as she started walking in the opposite direction.

"Have a good day," she said waving goodbye.

When class was over I went to Kacess'ion's school to pick her up. She was anxiously waiting on me with a group of her peers and a teacher. When she saw my car, she waved, said something to the teacher, and then ran over to the car.

"Hello mommy," she said leaning into the open passengers' window.

"Hello Boo, come on you know that you have to go to your singing lessons today."

"I thought that today was dance class," she said as she got into the car and threw her book bag in the back seat.

"Dance lessons are on Friday evenings."

"Mommy, can I go on a field trip next week?"

"Sure, where are you going?" I asked as I pushed a lock of her curls out of her face. It seemed like every day she was looking more and more like her father. I felt a tinge of sadness overcome me. There were times when Kacess'ion asked me about her father. I always made up excuses about why he was not able to come and see her.

"We are going to the farm to see real horses and cows," Kacess'ion said excitedly. I turned on the ignition and put the car in drive, as I started pulling off; I glanced in my rearview mirror and noticed a man taking pictures. He must be taking pictures of the school, I thought as I drove off.

I-20 had bumper-to-bumper traffic, as drivers were rushing to get home. After what seemed like forever, I finally got off on the M.L.K exit and started on my way to Kacess'ion's music lessons. It was obvious to me that Kacess'ion had a gift. She had a talent for carrying a melody. The music teacher loved to see her come; he told me that every so often he gets a child who is musically gifted. I enjoyed taking her to the school. Twice a year they put on shows, which allowed the children to show case their talents. It also helped them to get use to singing in front of an audience.

After her class was over, we jumped back on the freeway and went home. As we were entering the house, I heard the telephone ringing. I dropped my keys and purse on the desk beside my front door and rushed for the phone.

"Hello," I said breathlessly.

"Hello beautiful lady." It was David.

"Hello David, how are you doing?"

"I'm fine now that I hear your voice. How was your first day back at Grady?"

"Oh it was good. Everyone was coming up to me and asking me how I was doing."

"Well, you promised me I could take you out, how about this Saturday?"

"Yes, I would love to go out. I have not been out in a long time," I said with a smile.

"Great, I will see you on Saturday."

"Okay, I will see you then." I hung up the phone. Over the last two weeks since I had been released from the hospital, David had been coming over or calling me every day. Some nights we would be on the phone for hours.

I began preparing dinner and helping Kacess'ion with her homework, I was about to give Kacess'ion a bath when the telephone rang again. I went into my bedroom and picked up the telephone.

"Hello," I answered as I wiped my wet hands on a towel that I was holding.

The phone went dead. "It must have been a wrong number." I said aloud. I put the phone back on the hook and went back into the bathroom. After I finished giving Kacess'ion her bath, I tucked her in and read her a bedtime story. After I finished reading Cinderella, I took a shower and went to bed.

David arrived at my house at exactly 8:00 p.m. on Saturday. He looked so handsome in his expensive tailored suit. He would not tell me where we were going, he said it was a surprise. He told me that I needed to dress semiformal. It took me all week to find just the right dress. I ended up selecting a cream strapless dress made of silk from Macys.

"You look beautiful," he said with a look of appreciation on his face.

"Thank you, so do you. Let me call Rita before we leave. She is having a slumber party for all the school age children in her daycare. I just want to see if any other children showed up." I walked over to my phone and dialed her number.

"Hello," Rita answered.

"Hi Rita, its Karen, did any of the other children show up?"

"Oh yea six more kids came. We are about to make cookies."

"That's nice, would you please put Kacess'ion on the phone." I asked as I held a finger up to David letting him know to hold on a second. He waved for me to take my time and sat down on my couch.

"Hello mommy."

"Hello Boo. Are you having fun?"

"Yes, we are about to make ginger bread cookies, then Aunt Rita said we are going to play musical chairs. She said the winner gets a prize," she said excitedly.

"Okay, you have fun and I will see you tomorrow, don't forget to brush your teeth before you go to bed."

"Okay mommy I won't."

"Let me speak to Aunt Rita again."

"Okay, bye mommy."

"Bye Boo." Rita got back on the phone.

"So where are the two of you going?" She asked.

"I don't know he is not telling me, he said he wants it to be a surprise."

"Well, have fun."

"Thanks, you have fun too," I chuckled.

"Yea, I will probably be ready to pull my hair out by tomorrow," Rita laughed.

"See you tomorrow. I will try to get to your house early tomorrow morning."

"You know Kacess'ion is like one of my own, don't worry, take your time."

We hung up the phone, and then I walked over to the table by the door and picked up my keys.

"Okay I am ready now."

"Okay," he said as he got up and walked to the door.

He escorted me to a black play that was similar to the fairy tale story Cinderella. I was almost in tears toward the end of the play when the woman married her prince charming. I felt David squeeze my hand. I looked over at him and he smiled at me. After the play, he took me to a beautiful restaurant on the top floor of the Ritz-Carlton Hotel. We walked up to the front desk.

"Do you have reservations?" A short white man asked.

"Yes we do. It's under the name Smith," the man looked down a list until he found David's name.

"Please follow me," he said smiling, as he picked up two menus. We followed him to a small table in the corner of the room near the window. There was a lit candle on the table.

"This is so beautiful," I said as the host seated me.

"I have never been to a place like this before," I said as I picked up my menu. David reached across the table, gently touched my hand, and smiled.

"I have many more places I plan to show you Karen." The waiter walked up to the table.

"Can I get the two of you something to drink?" He asked as he pulled out his small note pad and pencil.

"Yes, we would like to have a bottle of your best Chablis," David replied as he stared at the menu.

"Okay, have you decided on what entree you would like to order or do you need more time?" The waiter asked.

"We will need more time, thank you," David replied. The waiter smiled and then walked away.

"I really don't drink very often," I said looking at the menu. The prices were so expensive; I almost decided to order just a salad. David must have been reading my mind. He gently touched my hand again.

"Don't worry about the prices, order whatever you want. The wine is to celebrate your recovery and our first date." When the waiter returned with our wine, I ordered steak, baked potato, and a salad. David ordered Shrimp and steak combination with a baked potato.

After the waiter took our order, he opened our wine and poured each of us a glass.

"Here's to our first date. I hope that there are many more to come," David said as he held up his glass for a toast. I picked up my glass and lightly tapped it against his. The wine actually tasted good. We chatted about everything from his latest delivery to Kacess'ion's singing lessons.

About twenty minutes later, the waiter returned with our order, the food was delicious. There was a large piano in the opposite corner of the room. One man was playing the piano and another was playing the saxophone. A few people were on the dance floor. When they began playing a familiar jazz tune, I started nodding my head to the music.

"Would you like to dance, after all the last time I asked you to dance you turned me down?" He said laughing. I knew that he was referring to the first time we met.

"Yes, I would like to dance," I said as I stood up. He walked around the table, took hold of my hand, and guided me to the dance floor. When he pulled me into his arms, I could feel his strong well-formed muscles. As we slow danced, I put my head on his chest. He kissed me on the forehead and then softly put his chin on my head. It felt so good to be held by him. We danced for what seemed like hours.

"Come on, let's go home," David said as he led me off the dance floor. We got our things; he paid for the meal, and left a large tip for the waiter. We left the restaurant and got on the elevator. When we walked out the building, a valet pulled up with David's Lexus. The valet opened the door for me and waited as I got in. I could feel the wine I had consumed starting to kick in, I was beginning to feel lightheaded. I was not so intoxicated however, that I did not realize that we were going in the wrong direction.

"Where are we going?" I asked.

"I wanted to show you where I live. Is that okay?" He asked as he quickly took his eyes off the road and glanced at me.

"Sure that's fine." I felt safe with him. I laid my head back on the headrest and closed my eyes, as I listened to Anita Baker's smooth voice singing, "You're my angel".

At some point during the ride, I must have fallen asleep.

"We are here," David said gently tapping my arm. When I opened my eyes and glanced around me, I gasped as we pulled into his driveway. I knew he had a nice place, but I never imagined it would look anything like this.

He owned a large yellow and brown, plantation style mansion. It had a large wrap around porch with a swing. The house sat on about an acre of land, the landscape was immaculate. There was a small pond in the front yard with lots of beautiful flowers and trees. I was very impressed.

"Before we go in the house would you like to sit on the swing with me?" He asked as he turned off the ignition.

"Sure," I said as I got out of the car. It was a beautiful warm night, the sky was so clear you could see the stars; there was not even one cloud in sight. We sat down on the swing and he pulled me into his arms.

"Karen, without a doubt, I know that I am falling in love with you. It's nothing that I planned or expected," he said as he held me close to him.

"I feel the same way. For so long I have been afraid to let anyone get too close to me. I was afraid that I would meet another man like Clyde." We sat in silence just holding each other, and then he stood up and led me into his house.

His home was just as beautiful inside as it was on the outside. It reminded me of Scarlet 'O'Hara and Rhett Butler's house in "Gone with the Wind." He walked me to the winding staircases that led to the second floor. He picked me up and quickly carried me up the long staircase to his bedroom, taking two steps at a time. He kicked his bedroom door open and laid me down on his large king size bed. I looked up and saw mirrors on top of the ceiling and behind the bed. I wondered what made him put mirrors in such an awkward place. The room had a large fireplace right across from the bed. He walked around the room lighting scented candles. Then he walked over to his stereo and turned on a Teddy Pendergrass CD. I smiled as I heard Teddy singing, "Turn off the lights and light a candle."

"It's been a long time for me," I said nervously. The last time that I was in a bedroom with a man I was being beaten and raped, I could feel my hands starting to sweat. He took off his jacket, tie and shirt, leaving on only his tee shirt and pants. He walked over to me and gently touched my cheeks with his hands.

"Karen, I promise I will not hurt you," he said as he sat down on the bed next to me. I closed my eyes as he began placing small feather like kisses on my face. He kissed my forehead, my eyelids, my nose, and then my mouth. His lips were so soft. I felt his tongue softly touch my lips, and then he began sucking on my top lip. He gently placed his hand on my thigh, slowly sliding his hand upward until he reached my breast. I was determined that I was going to make myself relax. He slid his hands to the back of my dress and slid down the zipper, and undid my strapless bra. As he pulled my dress down, he gently laid me back onto the bed. He let go of my lips and took one of my nipples into his mouth slowly sucking on them, I could feel myself getting wet.

I looked up at the ceiling and watched him through the mirrors. I began rubbing his baldhead and neck with my hands. He suddenly stood up and took off the rest of his clothes. My eyes grew wide as I looked at his large manhood. He pulled me by my hand and helped me to take off the rest of my clothing. Then he laid me back on the bed. He started devouring my breast again, sliding his tongue down my chest and making a path down to my belly button. When he reached my private spot and opened my legs, I grabbed his head.

"What are you doing?" I asked as I tried to scoot away from him. No man had ever put his mouth down there. He looked at me and smiled.

"Relax baby, this is all about you. This is what a man does when he wants to please his woman. I want to taste you," he whispered as he pulled me back toward him and lowered his head. I had never felt such ecstasy; I threw my head back and started moaning. I started feeling a tingling sensation that I had never felt before, a warm feeling started spreading all over my body down to my toes, my body started to tremble. I screamed and grabbed David's head as a wonderful explosive feeling took over my body.

He continued until he had drunk all my juices, then he picked me up and straddled me putting my legs around his waist and guiding my arms around his neck. I felt him softly enter me, and then he walked over to the wall and held me up against it as he began slowly and softly thrusting his large shaft in and out of my wet womanhood. I could still feel my body tingling from the orgasm I had just had.

"Oh you feel so good," he whispered in my ear. Then he carried me back over to the bed and laid me down, he reentered me starting slow. It was as if he was trying to savor every moment.

He continued kissing me, occasionally he would stop so that he did not climax too quickly and we would change positions. Our bodies were wet with perspiration.

When he could not hold out any longer, he began thrusting harder and faster. I wrapped my legs around his back. Finally, when I thought I could not handle any more of his passionate loving, I heard him whimper then he fell gently on top of me, the perspiration from his head slid down onto my shoulder.

"You are so beautiful, I love you Karen," he said as he lay on top of me breathing hard. After a few minutes, he got up and ran us a bubble bath. He took some of the candles into the bathroom, and then led me into the large bathroom. He helped me into the large whirlpool tub, and then stepped into the tub and sat down behind me.

The water felt so nice and warm, I laid my head against his chest and relaxed. After soaking for a while, we took turns washing each other off. When we were finished, David helped me out of the tub, toweled me off, put lotion on my body, and then gave me one of his shirts to wear. He put on a white robe and left the room. When he came back, he had a big bowel of grapes and two sodas. He handed me the tray and then sat down on the bed.

"I have never had a man make love to me like that before. I never knew it could be that good. I use to see sex as a horrible and dirty thing. Tonight I learned that it can be a beautiful experience." I said as I rubbed my hand over his baldhead. He leaned over and kissed me on the lips.

"I am glad that I was able to please you."

We fed each other grapes and talked about what we hoped our future would be like together. We made love again before finally falling asleep in each other's arms.

CHAPTER 19

I woke up the next morning to the smell of bacon. I looked over and saw that David was not in the bed. I got up and went into the bathroom, took a quick shower, and then I put on his bathrobe. As I was walking out of the bathroom, David opened the door, holding a tray.

"Good morning, beautiful lady," he said as he put the tray down on the nightstand. He had a towel around his waist. He had such a muscular and well-toned body for a man his age. I smiled as I sat down on the bed.

"Mmm, something smells good."

"I made it just for you," he replied as he picked the tray back up and laid it across my lap. He cooked bacon, eggs, grits with cheese, and toast. The tray had a beautiful red rose and a big glass of orange juice on it.

"Where's yours?" I asked as I enjoyed the savoring smell.

"I am going to go and get mine; it's on the breakfast counter in the kitchen. I just wanted to serve you first, go ahead and start eating I'll be right back." He turned and walked out the door. I looked at the food, said a quick prayer, and then began eating. He had cooked the eggs just as I liked them, sunny side up. A few minutes later, he returned with his own tray and sat down on the bed. After we finished eating, we laid back on the bed.

"David, what made you put mirrors on your ceiling?" I asked as I stared at our reflections.

"I guess I am not the first woman to get special treatment." I felt a tinge of jealousy stab at my heart. I did not want to think of another woman getting this same attention. He glanced at the ceiling and then turned toward me, giving me a very serious look.

"Karen, I am not going to lie to you and tell you that I am a saint or that I have been celibate since my ex-wife and I divorced, I have dated quite a few women. The one thing I will say is that none of them have had the effect on me that you do."

"Do you really mean that, or are you just trying to make me feel better about giving it up on the first date?" I chuckled. I thought about my grandmother, she would have had a heart attack if she knew that I was sleeping with a man that I was not married to.

"Even if you had told me that you didn't want to make love last night that would not have changed the way I feel about you. I have never felt this strong about anyone other than my ex-wife," he said gently stroking my arm.

"I have only had one other man in my life. When I was with Clyde, he made me feel like his sexual property. I promised myself that I would never allow another man to treat me that way. I was determined to remain single for the rest of my life." I said as I got up and started putting on my clothes.

"Well I am glad that you finally gave me a chance," he said as he got up and walked over to me. He put his arms around my waist, and began placing feather like kisses me on my neck. He led me back to the bed and began kissing me again.

I felt a little sore from making love twice the night before, but I welcomed him warmly.

Once we were both dressed, I called Rita to let her know that I was going to stop at home for a minute and then I would be on my way to get Kacess'ion.

As we pulled into my driveway, I had a funny feeling that something was not right.

When I walked to the front door, I saw that my front window had been broken out and was slightly open. David must have seen the window at the same time because he got out of the car and walked up to the front door.

"David, someone has broken into my house. I don't want to go inside incase the person is still here," I whispered. We got back in the car and David called the police on his cell phone.

"Why are all these horrible things happening to me?" I asked as I stared at my house. It took about ten minutes for the police to arrive. David got out of the car and met them at the front door. They drew their weapons and pushed the front door open. After about fifteen minutes, they came back outside and motioned for us to come to the door.

"Ma'am, whoever broke in is gone, but it looks like they made a big mess. You will need to go through all your things and record what's missing while we fill out the report," the black officer said as he walked toward his police car. I walked into my house and gasped, broken glass was everywhere, photographs were torn to pieces and lying all over the floor. I walked to my room, there were papers lying everywhere, and my clothes were all over the floor. It almost looked like the person who broke into my house became very angry and started throwing things. The one thing that was unusual was that my TV's and VCR were still there. After taking a trip around the house, I could not point out one thing in particular that was missing.

"It doesn't look like they took anything," I said as I walked back into the living room where the officers and David were standing.

"That's odd, all of these TVs and VCRs that they could have taken. Are you sure this was not done by someone that you know?" The officer asked.

"I don't know anyone who would have done this," I said as I sat down on the couch.

"Well, if you find anything missing, just come down to the police station and report it. If you have any questions just call this number."

The police officer handed me a sheet of paper with a number written on it. Then he handed me the report sheet and had me sign it. After the police left, I turned to David with tears in my eyes.

"David, I need a weapon. If I had been here when they broke in, I would not have been able to protect myself. I want you to take me to buy a gun." At first, he did not say anything, and then he turned to me and shook his head.

"Lets go and get one now. It will take a few days before they will actually give it to you. I will teach you how to use it. I think it would be wise for you and Kacess'ion to stay with me for a while, just in case this person decides to come back and get the things he left."

"Okay, let me get some clothes and a few personal items for me and Kacess'ion." I said as I walked to my bedroom. After leaving my house, he took me to the gun store and helped me pick out a 9mm Beretta. After we filled out the registration form, the clerk informed me that if everything checked out I would be able to pick up the gun next week. After leaving the gun store, we went to Rita's house. When we pulled up to her house, the children were playing with a ball on the front lawn. As soon as Kacess'ion saw David's car she ran up to us.

"Hello mommy, Hello Mr. Smith," she said with a big smile. It was obvious that she had been having a lot of fun with her friends. I got out of the car and gave her a big hug.

"Hello Boo." I said.

"Hello Kacess'ion how are you doing. Did you and your friends have a lot of fun last night at the slumber party?" David asked as he shut his car door and started walking toward her.

"Yes, we made cookies, and we played games, and Aunt Rita let us put on makeup."

"Wow, it sounds like you really did have a lot of fun." I said as I kissed her on the cheek. When we walked into the house, Rita and Monica were sitting at the kitchen table playing a game of spades.

"Hello David, hello Karen," Monica said a she arranged the cards in her hand.

"Hello Dr. Smith, hey what's up Karen, how was your night," Rita asked as she threw out a card.

"Hello ladies." David replied.

"Hey what's up, you guys will never guess what happened someone broke into my house," I said as I sat at the table.

"Someone broke into your house?" Rita and Monica said at the same time with a look of disbelief.

"The most unusual thing is they didn't steal anything," I said as I took a piece of peppermint candy out of the candy jar and put it into my mouth.

"They didn't take anything? They didn't take any of your TV's," Monica asked.

"Nope, at first I thought maybe it was a crack head, but a crack head would have taken all the TVs and VCRs that he could find." David said as he sat down at the breakfast bar.

"Kacess'ion and I are going to stay at David's house for a little while."

"That's smart, it's best that you and Kacess'ion are not there in case they decide to come back. What did the police say?" Rita asked as she began shuffling the playing cards.

"They told me that if I find something missing, that I need to go down and report it. They tried dusting for fingerprints, but were not able to get anything they said that the person must have been wearing gloves."

"Did they do a lot of damage?" Monica asked.

"They tore my house apart, its going to take me days to get it all straightened up."

"Do you want some help?" Rita asked.

"Yes, I could use some help." I said as I stood up from the table.

"Okay, we will call Jessica and see when she is off, and then we will all come over and help. If the five of us work together, we can have your house straighten up in no time." Monica replied as she picked up her hand and glanced over her cards.

"Well, we are about to go, thanks Rita for keeping Kacess'ion."

"No problem, call me if you need anything. See you later David."

"Goodbye ladies," David said as he followed me out of the kitchen.

When we left Rita's house, David took us to Dairy Queen for ice cream then we went back to his house. I was so thankful that he was going to let us stay with him. I did not feel good about going back to my house.

FEAR

PART V

Whenever you feel fear, just remember that God is near.

When you are afraid, do not run away.

This is the time you should stop and pray.

God will lead you the rest of the way.

God has equipped you with all the spiritual weapons you need.

Just speak his word and you will see.

All of your demons will flee.

CHAPTER 20

My friends helped me clean my house and David paid to have a new window put in. After a few months Kacess'ion and I moved back home. David had offered to let us stay longer, but I did not want to become a burden. I felt like he had already gone out of his way for my daughter and me. Kacess'ion had grown to love him. When he returned home from work, if she was still awake, he would sit with me while I read her a bedtime story. Every other weekend he took us out to eat and to a movie. I could tell that he would make a very good father.

The man who attacked me was given a sentence of twenty years to life for attempted murder. He was extradited to Ohio after the trial to face more charges. During the trial, I finished my internship at Grady and started working full time on their seven to three-shift on the obstetrics ward. I also started doing PRN work, in the emergency room. Everything was returning to normal and I was starting to feel relaxed again until the day I received a call on my cell phone from Kacess'ion's principal.

"Hello," I answered as I lowered the volume on my car radio.

"Ms. King, this is Mr. Wright, the principal at Kingsville Elementary."

Kacess'ion hardly ever got sick, and when she did, the principal never called. I knew it had to be serious. "Is something wrong?" I asked.

"Well ma'am, I hate to disturb you, but this afternoon a man came to the school and tried to withdraw Kacess'ion out of class. He said that he was her father." I felt like my heart had skipped a beat. I could not have heard him correctly.

"Her father tried to take her out of school?" I asked in disbelief.

"Yes ma'am, but we didn't let her go with him. The man became very irate with me, but I let him know that unless his name is on the emergency list, we could not release her to him. He was pretty upset when he left." Mr. Wright stated.

"Okay, I am on my way!" I hung up the phone before he was able to say goodbye.

"Oh my God, he found me." I said aloud my heart started beating fast and I could feel myself break out into a sweat, I started speeding. I knew I had to get us out of Georgia. When I reached the school, I ran to the office and took Kacess'ion by the hand, grabbed her book bag and left the building. I was so scared. I kept glancing around me as we got into the car, trying to see if I could see him.

"Mommy, what's wrong?" Kacess'ion asked as I sped away from the school.

"Nothing sweet heart," I gently pulled her hair out of her face. I drove to Jessica's house, jumped out of the car and practically pulled Kacess'ion out of the car with her seat belt still on. After I unhooked her seatbelt, I took hold of her hand and ran to the front door, knocking frantically. Jessica's husband answered the door.

"Hey Mike, is Jessica here," I asked breathing hard.

"Yes, she is in the kitchen, are you okay?" He asked frowning. I did not stop to answer him, I ran to the kitchen, practically dragging Kacess'ion with me.

"He found me Jessica!" I said breathlessly as tears started flowing down my face.

I walked over to her table and sat down.

"Who found you?" She asked. She put down the knife that she had been using to cut vegetables and walked over to me, putting her hand on my shoulder.

"Clyde, he tried to withdraw Kacess'ion out of school today!" I said hysterically.

"Calm down honey." She said as she handed me a Kleenex. Then she turned to Kacess'ion.

"Baby, go outside and play with the kids while I talk to your mama."

"What's wrong with mommy?" She yelled. I knew I was making her upset because she had started crying. Jessica gave her a Kleenex and then led her out of the kitchen. When she came back in the room, she sat down next to me and took hold of my hand.

"I have to leave Georgia. I can't stay here anymore!" I said crying.

"Karen, just calm down, you do not have to leave Georgia."

"Jessica you don't understand. I cannot stay here anymore. Clyde is going to try to take Kacess'ion away from me. Will you watch Kacess'ion while I go to my house and get a few of our things?" I asked frantically.

"Sure Karen, but you cannot keep running from him. Honey, you know my husband is a lawyer. We can help you." I shook my head; she just did not understand what type of man Clyde was. Clyde knew too many people in high places. I stood up, grabbed my purse and keys and ran out of the house. All I knew was that my life in Georgia was over, we had to leave and it had to be tonight. Once we reached our new destination, I planned to call David and let him know what had happened.

By the time I got to my house, I could feel my heart beating fast. I jumped out of my car and ran up the walkway. I unlocked my door and threw my keys on the table next to the front door. I walked into the living room and stopped dead in my tracks.

Clyde was sitting with his legs crossed and his arms stretched out on the back of my couch. I thought I was going to faint right there on the spot.

"Well hello baby, long time no see," he smirked. He had a wicked smile on his face.

"Clyde, how did you get into my house?" I asked in a low, shaky voice. He moved his arm from behind the couch and tossed my spare set of keys on the table. After the break in, I forgot to search for the spare keys.

"You broke into my house?" I asked in shock.

"Where is my daughter?" He asked standing up and walking toward me.

"She is over a friend's house. I advise you to leave before I call the police." I said as I walked to the table and picked up the telephone.

"Did you forget that I am the police?" He asked as he walked over to the wall and snatched the phone cord out of the jack.

"I came here to take you and my daughter back home."

"How did you find me?" I asked with a look of horror on my face.

"Well it seems that you had an incident with a man who was on the most wanted list in Ohio. When he attacked you, it made news and the officials in Georgia notified our precinct. I have had a private detective looking for you for the last two years. I had almost given up hope. I guess I should thank the man who attacked you for helping me to find you," he said as he started walking toward me.

"We are not going back to Ohio. Our marriage is over Clyde," I said in a shaky voice taking a few steps back toward the front door.

"Oh so you plan on leaving me for the fancy doctor? He asked in a sarcastic voice.

"How long have you been having me watched?" I thought about the day that I saw the man taking pictures at Kacess'ion's school.

"Long enough, I told you once before that if you ever tried to leave me for another man that I would kill you, you can either come with me willingly or I will do to you what I did to your cousin and raise our daughter by myself," he replied with a smirk look on his face. I almost choked. I could not believe my ears.

"You killed Linda!" I screamed. I ran toward the door but he grabbed me and pushed me up against the wall. He tightly grasped my cheeks with his hand, slightly covering my mouth. He had his face so close to mine that I could smell the alcohol on his breath.

"I told the bitch that if she didn't tell me where my child was, that she was going to disappear. For some reason she did not take me seriously. I do not understand why women do not listen. I tried to tell my first wife that the only way she was going to leave me was in a body bag. She did not listen either, decided she did not want to be with me anymore. She tried to leave me for another man. I put both of them out of their misery," he said with a sickening laugh. I knew I had to get away from him at that second, I knew that he was planning to kill me. When we were still together, he told me that his wife and her friend had died in an accidental fire.

I kneed him in the groin; he yelled out in pain and released me. I tried to run for the door but he ran after me, tackling me to the floor like a football player, knocking over the table beside my front door. He straddled me, and started punching me in my face with his fist. I screamed as I tried to defend myself but he was too strong. Then he put his hands around my neck and started squeezing. I could not breathe. At first I tried to scratch at his hands, then I flung my arms wildly around on the floor, my hand grazed over my keys and I felt the bottle of Mace. I grabbed the bottle, flipped the top, and sprayed it in his face. He let go of my neck as he yelled and wiped at his eyes. I jumped up and ran toward my bedroom. I slammed the door shut and locked it, picked up the phone and dialed 911.

"This is 911, what's your emergency?" A female dispatcher answered.

"Please hurry. My husband is trying to kill me!" I screamed. Then I heard Clyde kicking the door.

"Open this door bitch; I am going to kill you just like I killed your cousin!" He yelled. I knew the door did not have a strong lock and that he was going to get in before the police arrived. I dropped the phone on the bed, reached under my mattress, and pulled out the gun that David had taken me to buy. I removed the safety lock as David had instructed. I was cocking the gun when Clyde burst into the room, knocking the weak door off its hinges. I screamed at the loud noise. When I saw the knife he was holding in his hand, I pointed the gun at him. My hand was shaking violently; he looked at me in surprise and then smiled.

"Put the gun down, you don't have the guts to shoot me Karen," He said in a low voice as he started walking slowly toward me.

"You had better stop or I will shoot you!" I yelled as I wiped the blood from my nose with the back of my free hand.

"Why would you want to hurt me, I am your husband and I love you?" He said in a low voice, still walking toward me with the knife in his hand.

"You don't know what love is!" I screamed. I closed my eyes and fired the gun. My intention had been to shoot him in his leg and scare him. At first, I thought I missed him because when I opened my eyes he was just standing there with a surprised look on his face. Then he dropped the knife and grabbed his chest before falling to the floor. I did not move I just sat there in a daze, holding the gun in my hand.

A few minutes later, I heard the front door burst in and men yelling "police!" I did not move, I could not move, I was in shock. When the police officers entered my room, they saw Clyde on the floor and the gun in my hand.

"Drop the gun lady!" The black police officer yelled as he pointed his gun at me. I released the gun, letting it fall to the floor. One police officer kneeled down next to Clyde, pulled out his radio and yelled for an ambulance. The other police officer ran over to me, pushed me onto the bed on my stomach, put his knee in my back, while pulling my arms behind me and putting handcuffs on both of my wrist. Then he ran over to Clyde and got down on his knees next to the other officer.

"I don't feel a pulse!" The white officer yelled. The black officer started CPR, pumping Clyde's chest while the other officer began giving him rescue breathes.

A few minutes later, the paramedics ran into the room. The paramedics worked on Clyde for about fifteen minutes before pronouncing him dead. The white officer walked over to me and pulled me off the bed, pushing me toward the bedroom door.

"You are under arrest." Was all I heard him say, as he was reading me my rights, I just kept staring at Clyde's lifeless body on the floor. I could not believe that I had just killed my husband. I started crying as the police officer grabbed my arm and pulled me to the front door and out onto the porch. All my neighbors were standing on their porches, and on the sidewalk, watching as the police officer put me in the back of his police car.

Clyde had killed my cousin, his first wife, and his wife's lover. I knew that he was mean and cruel, but I never pictured him as a murderer. I laid my head back against the seat as the police officer got into the car and started the ignition.

CHAPTER 21

The police officers drove me to Fulton County Jail. He pulled the car into a small area; I saw gates come down in front and behind the police car. I guess the gates were to make sure that an inmate did not try to escape. The black police officer pulled me out of the car and led me to a steel door. We waited as the deputy inside a windowed office pushed a button that opened the doors. Once we entered, the iron doors closed behind us. I jumped as I heard the door close with a loud bang.

The police officer made me face the wall as he took off my handcuffs. A female officer searched my body and my belongings for weapons and drugs. I felt very uncomfortable and violated when the deputy searched me. After they finished searching me I was told to take a seat in a row of chairs with about six other women. The large room was about the size of a gym. I glanced behind me and saw holding cells; each cell had fifteen to twenty men inside. There were also rows of men sitting in chairs; in the middle of the room was a large tower where a deputy was sitting. Directly in front of me were sectional dividers. Each section had a computer, a desk and a sign above it. One sign said Booking, another sign said Pretrial, and then down a ways was an office that said Medical Screening.

I sat there for what seemed like hours before the deputy sitting behind the booking desk called my name. A deputy walked over to me and pointed to the chair in front of booking. I got up, walked to the chair, and sat down.

A black female deputy asked me demographic questions, and then told me to go sit back down and wait to be finger printed and to have my picture taken.

"What are you in here for?" A white woman asked as I sat back down. I just looked at her. I really did not want to talk about what just happened. She must have sensed that I was not going to answer her because she started talking without waiting for me to reply.

"My boyfriend got mad at me because I used the last shot of heroin and tried to beat me up, so I stabbed him in the chest with a fork," she said slowly as if she was still high. She looked to be in her forty's, her brunette hair looked like it had not been washed in a month and she had a foul odor. It was obvious that she lived on the streets.

"I sure hope that they give me some methadone when I get over to medical screening, that's what they gave me last month. I can already feel my high coming down," she said as she looked toward the medical screening office. I just looked at her without responding. I glanced around the room; I could not believe how many African Americans and Mexicans were in jail. There were rows of them waiting to go through the same process as I was going through. Most of the men did not look much older than eighteen years old. After the deputy took my photograph, the deputy placed me in a cell with six other women.

"Hey deputy, I got high blood pressure and I have not had my medicine in two days. My head is hurting really bad." An old black woman said to the deputy who put me in the cell. The deputy walked away, I wondered if she had even heard the woman.

"You bitch!" The woman yelled when the cell door closed in her face. She walked back over to the bench and sat down next to me.

"Maybe she didn't hear you." I said. I felt sorry for her.

"That bitch heard me; she has had it in for me all night. I guess she is mad because I cussed her out about giving us those same old nasty sandwiches. I have been in this damn cell for two days and all I have been eating are bologna sandwiches," she said wrinkling up her face.

"Hell, I heard some of those guys over there have been down here for five days," a young black girl said.

"Damn, I don't want to be down here that long, they don't have any beds, it's hard on my back trying to sleep on this bench." The old black woman complained as she lay on the cold bench, curled into a ball, and pulled her coat over her knees.

"I heard that women are considered priority over the men. I have been down here since last night. I have not been to see the doctor yet. I cannot stand coming to this damn jail. They are so slow." A middle-aged white woman complained.

I just looked at her. She was a heavyset woman, she looked like she might have been about forty-five or fifty years old. She had scars that looked like old cut wounds. I could not understand why she kept coming back to jail if she knew how bad it was.

About two hours later, a deputy and some trustee's handed us sandwiches, milk, and oranges. I did not have an appetite. I had been feeling nauseous all day.

"Are you are going to eat that?" One of the women asked me.

"No, I am not feeling too good right now." I said as I looked at the food.

"Can I have it?" She asked holding out her hand.

"Sure." I replied handing her my meal. I looked around the cell. There were no beds just stone benches. There was only one toilet in the corner of the room. Was I really supposed to use the bathroom in front of all these women? I shuddered at the thought and prayed that I would not have to go to the bathroom anytime soon.

At some point, I must have fallen asleep. I dreamed that I was back at my house and Clyde was choking me, he was laughing at me and had red eyes like the devil. I jumped up. I was breathing hard. I looked around me and remembered where I was. I looked at my watch. It was 10:30 at night. I had been in jail since 12:30 that afternoon. The cell door opened and three more women came in and sat down. One woman looked directly into my face. She kept staring at me as if she knew me.

"I know who you are; you are here for killing a police officer from Ohio it has been on the news all day," the old woman blurted out. I did not say anything. I just looked at her. By this time, I knew that David and my friends knew that I was in jail. Rita never missed the six 'o'clock news. We use to laugh at her all the time, she could be in the middle of cooking, playing cards, or giving kids a bath, when six o'clock hit, everything else had to wait. Thank God, I had taken Kacess'ion over to Jessica's house. I would not have been able to forgive myself if she had witnessed her father's murder. I knew that would have scarred her for life.

There was a lot of commotion going on in the lobby, we all stood up and went to the cell door. There was a black man yelling that he had full-blown AIDS, and he was going to kill someone. Every time one of the deputies would try to get near him, he would spit at them. All the deputies seemed to be scared. The man pulled out his manhood and urinated on a shirt he held in his hand and began wiping it on the windows. The commotion continued until one of the young deputies snuck up behind the man and knocked him to the floor. Then the other deputies came over with gloves on and put him in a cell. We all sat back down on the benches.

"Man, but it's some crazy ass people in Atlanta," one black girl chuckled. I listened as the women exchanged stories about their experiences in Fulton County Jail. Two of the women even knew each other from another time when they were both in jail at the same time. I shook my head with sadness. These women had so much that they could be doing with their lives. I wondered what made them take this road. I guess I could not really say but so much since, I was sitting in here for killing my husband. I thought about what I could have done differently. I knew that I reacted in fear. I believed that he was going to kill me. I wish that I had not closed my eyes when I fired the gun. If the bullet had hit him in the leg or arm instead of his chest, he would still be alive and I would not be sitting here.

I must have nodded back to sleep. I heard someone yelling my name, and then I felt someone shove me. I jumped up.

"King?" The short white deputy yelled.

"Yes!" I yelled as I quickly walked to the cell door.

"They want you in pretrial," she replied as she yelled for the guard in the tower to open our cell door. I walked to the pretrial station.

"You have been charged with murder. We are unable to give you a bond. You will have to go before the judge."

"When will I get to see the judge?" I asked.

"I cannot tell from looking at this screen," she replied as she typed on the computer.

"Well can I at least use the telephone, I have been here for hours and I have not been allowed to use the phone."

"Sure go ahead," The deputy stated. I got up and walked over to the phone booth. I reached into my pocket and took out my change. I had enough for two phone calls. I decided to call David first.

"Hello?" He answered the phone on the first ring.

"David." That is all I could get out before I burst into tears.

"Oh baby. I heard what happened. Do not worry we are going to get you out. I called to find out if you had a bond and they said you had to see the judge first. Mike has already notified his firm. They are going to get you the best lawyer Atlanta has," he said in a soothing voice.

"I can't afford to pay for a lawyer." I sobbed.

"Baby, that's what you have a man for. Do not worry about money. You let me worry about that. You just concentrate on keeping yourself calm. Besides, you know that Jessica's husband has connections. Mike already told me that his firm would not charge the regular price for services."

"Thank you," I said trying to calm myself down.

"I just wish I could have been there for you. The clerk said I can't come and see you until you are booked in and your visitation day arrives."

"David, Clyde is the one who broke into my house. He also confessed to killing my cousin Linda, and his first wife and her lover. He told me that if I did not leave with him that he was going to kill me. I did not mean to kill him. I was just going to shoot him in the leg. But when I saw the knife in his hand, I panicked." I sobbed. I kept wiping my nose with the back of my hand and wiping the drainage from my nose onto my pants' leg.

"Oh baby, I wish I could be there right now to hold you. Do not worry about anything. You are not alone. You have people here who love you, to back you up. You also have me." He said forcefully into the phone.

"Yes I know," I whispered.

"What about Kacess'ion?" I asked.

"Jessica said she is going to take her back over Rita's house tomorrow. Rita will be taking care of her until you get out. I gave Rita a thousand dollars today to take care of her. She really didn't want to take the money but I insisted," he replied.

"David you didn't have to do that," I said. I was surprised that he had given Rita that much money.

"Of course I did, you are my woman, aren't you?" He asked.

"Yes," I replied with a smile. It was the first time I had smiled all day. A deputy came up behind me.

"It's time to get off the phone," the deputy said in a firm voice.

"I have to go baby, I love you," I said and then hung up the phone.

"Can I please make just one more call? I just found out where my daughter is going to be staying while I am in jail, I just want to call and check on her." She looked like she was about to say no but then had second thoughts.

"You have ten minutes, make it quick," she said and walked away. I put more coins into the phone and dialed Rita's number.

"Hello?" She answered.

"Hey Rita, its Karen."

"Girl, I heard about what happened. Do not worry about a thing. We are going to get you out of there. Do not worry about Kacess'ion. Jessica is going to bring her over to my house tomorrow on her way to work. David paid me a thousand dollars to keep Kacess'ion. I kept trying to tell him that he did not have to pay me. You know that Kacess'ion is like one of my own."

"I know. I just want to say thank you Rita. I also wanted to ask you a favor." I said anxiously. The deputy seemed to be standing behind me listening to my conversation. I knew I was going to have to get off the phone soon.

"Take down this number, I want you to call my grandmother in Ohio and let her know what has happened. Tell her to get in touch with Uncle Jason. I need to speak with him."

"Okay, hold on while I get a pen." There was a brief silence on the other end of the phone.

"Okay, I have a pen go ahead with the number," Rita said breathlessly as if she had been running.

"Okay its 614-777-9999," Rita repeated the number back to me to make sure that she had all of the digits; she promised me that she would call first thing in the morning. Then we hung up.

"Okay, let's go ladies, its time to go back to your cell," the deputy said impatiently. I walked back to the cell and sat down on the bench.

"Thank you God for David and all my other friends, please forgive me for all my sins, and please forgive me for killing Clyde," I said silently.

When I was a little girl, my grandmother told me that no sin was any better or worse than another sin. She told me Jesus died on the cross to cover our sins and that if you ask God for forgiveness for something bad you have done, he will always forgive you.

CHAPTER 22

It was early the next morning before I finally went to the medical screening office. The deputy came into the cell and handed me a cup.

"You need to urinate in this cup; medical needs you to give them some urine before they will screen you," she stated. I had been holding my urine all day trying to avoid using the toilet that was in the cell. As much as I hated going to the bathroom in front of everyone I was also relieved. I was starting to feel like my bladder was going to burst. I filled up the container and then put it inside the small biohazard bag the deputy had given me. I tapped on the cell door to let her know that I was finished. When the deputy heard me, she turned around and yelled for the tower to open our cell door, and then she led me over to the office that said medical screening.

"Sit right here and wait for them to call your name!" The deputy demanded.

I sat down and put the bag with the urine in it on the floor next to my chair. There were three other women sitting in front of the medical screening office. Across from us were holding cells filled with men. They were hollering at us, trying to get our attention.

"Hey chocolate lady, when I get out of here you and I can hook up!" One inmate yelled at me. I looked at him and rolled my eyes.

"You guys had better shut up before we throw you asses in the rubber room!" One deputy yelled. I had never heard of the rubber room before.

"What is the rubber room?" I asked the woman sitting next to me.

"Oh, that's the room where they take people when they are going to beat them up or spray them with Mace," the woman replied laughing.

The men must have known what the rubber room was because they stopped talking to us.

I sat in front of the medical office for about an hour before a short black nurse with curls came to the door and called my name.

"Karen King!" She yelled.

"That's me," I said standing up.

"Do you have your urine?" She asked with a disgusted look on her face.

Yes," I replied picking up the bag and showing it to her.

"All right come on in," she said as she walked back into the room. I followed her into the office. There were four desks in the room and a scale. Beside each desk was a blue chair that the inmates sat in.

"I need you to take the urine out of the bag, put this name tag on the outside of the container, then put it back inside the bag, and stick it on the red bio-hazard trash can in the lab room." I took the sticker from her and put it on the outside of the container. Then I went to the small room located inside the office. There was a nurse inside drawing blood from another female inmate; I put the urine on the red trashcan.

"Come and get on this scale so that I can weigh you," the nurse said impatiently. I stepped on the scale, after she weighed me; I followed her past three other inmates to her desk in the back of the room and sat down.

She pulled out a blood pressure cuff and took my vital signs, then began asking me questions as she wrote the information on a pink intake screening form.

"When was your last menstrual period?" She asked as she filled out my form. Her question took me by surprise. I could not remember when I had my last period. With all the things that had been happening in my life over the last few months, I had not been keeping up with it.

After calculating the time in my head, I realized that I had not had a period in two months.

"I have not had a period in about two months," I replied. She looked at me with raised eyebrows.

"Are your cycles usually irregular?" She asked. My period had never skipped a month before. The only other time I could remember not having a period was when I was pregnant with Kacess'ion.

"No, they are usually on time, but I have been under a lot of stress lately. I guess my body has gotten thrown off course." I replied. The nurse turned toward the lab room.

"Hey Melinda, check Karen King's urine for pregnancy." She said to the woman in the lab. Then she turned back around and continued with the screening process.

"Do you have HIV or AIDS?" She asked as she continued to write.

"No."

"Have you ever been tested?" She asked.

"Yes, I had an AIDS test about five years ago, when I was pregnant with my daughter."

"Have you ever had a Tuberculosis test?" The nurse asked.

"Yes," I replied.

"Was it negative or positive?"

"It was negative; I had to get one done before I could start work," I said as I glanced at one of the female inmates that stood up to leave the office.

"Do you drink or do drugs?" she asked sarcastically.

"No."

"Are you currently taking any medications?"

"No."

"Karen King's pregnancy test came back positive." The lab woman named Melinda said as she stood in the doorway. I turned around in shock.

"Are you sure?" I asked.

"Yes I'm sure I checked it twice," she replied.

"What a way to find out that you are expecting," the nurse laughed. She continued screening me, and then she instructed me to go into the lab. Melinda took some blood from me and performed a TB test.

"Congratulations on your pregnancy, remember that regardless of what you are going through right now, children are a blessing from God," she said as I walked out of the lab.

"Thank you," I replied. Everyone else at the jail had been so mean to me. I was surprised to meet someone with compassion.

"Go back out there and sit down, the deputy will be over to get you," the nurse stated. I left the office and went back to the chair I had been sitting in. I could not believe that I was pregnant by David. Neither one of us ever bothered to use protection. I was not sure if I was happy or not. The thought of having a baby in prison made me depressed. The deputy finally came and retrieved all of us that had been through medical screening.

The deputies took us to a restroom and instructed us to shower and change into blue prison uniforms. We took an elevator to the third floor, and then we were placed into another holding cell. I sat there for about two hours before the doctor pulled me out. After he gave me a quick physical, he wrote an order for prenatal vitamins and then sent me back to the holding cell. A few hours later, I went to the female inmate zone with a group of women.

The zone looked like a big auditorium with a large TV hanging from the ceiling and metal picnic tables in the center of the room. There were holding cells leading all the way down the length of the room and a long metal staircase that led to another set of cells on the second floor. The deputy led me to a cell that I would be sharing with another female inmate. She handed me a bag that had a pillowcase, sheets, covers, toiletries, a cup, and eating utensils in it. I walked into the cell and threw my things on the bottom bunk.

"What's up young cat, my name is Kim, what's yours?" My roommate asked while looking me up and down.

"Karen," I replied as I sat down on my bunk.

"I saw you on the news. You killed your husband didn't you?" She asked as she peeled an orange that she was holding. I did not say anything. I just nodded my head yes.

"I feel for you girl, if they find you guilty you are going to do some serious time. They do not have too much pity on you when you kill a cop. If you are lucky, they might only give you fifteen years. I had a friend that killed her husband and they gave her twenty-five years to life. The man had been beating the shit out of her for years, but they say she planned it. So they charged her with first degree murder." She said as she took a bite of her orange.

"I'm in here for burglary. My old man and I robbed a liqueur store. He is in jail too. They caught us on video." She said as she took another bite of her orange before throwing the rest in a bag. Kim was a black woman; she looked like she was about thirty-five years old. She had a long scar down her neck and bags under her eyes.

"Oh." I replied. I was not in the mood to talk, especially after she shared the information about her friend with me. I lay back on my bunk and stared at the ceiling. I could not believe that I was pregnant. I put my hands to my stomach.

"God, please don't let me have to go through my pregnancy in jail. Please don't let them find me guilty of murder." I prayed silently. I knew that I had killed Clyde, but it was self-defense, not murder.

CHAPTER 23

I was in jail for about a week before David was able to come and
see me. My heart swelled with love when I saw him sitting on the other
side of the plastic window. When he saw me, he smiled and picked up
the phone as I sat down in the chair across from him.

"Hello baby, how are you doing, they are not treating you too bad
in here are they?" He said into the phone as he looked at me with sad
eyes.

"I'm okay. I found out some surprising news when I went through
medical screening." I said as I took a deep breath. I did not want to
hold the pregnancy a secret. I figured I might as well let him know
right away.

"Really, what did you find out?" He asked with a raised brow.

"They told me that I am pregnant." A look of surprise covered his
face.

"Don't worry baby. We are going to get you out of here. There is no
way you are going to be carrying my baby in jail. You should have your
first court date by the 23rd of next month.

"Why is it going to take so long for me to see the judge?" I asked.

"The clerk told me that the County is really backed up. They are
having problems with their computer systems. The 23rd was the soonest
date that they could get you before a judge." David replied frowning.

"When will I meet my lawyer?" I asked.

"Your lawyer will be here to see you next week to go over your case.
We have already given him a lot of information. Mrs. Francis has been
to see him also." He said with a serious look on his face. I smiled at the
thought of Mrs. Francis. She did not play when it came to her girls.

Whenever they needed her, she was always there, even once they had left the house and was out on their own.

"The lawyers' name is Bob Samuels; he is from Mike's law firm. He owes Mike a favor so he is willing to take the case for a fraction of what he normally charges. He told me that once he gets all the information together and goes to the judge that the judge would probably rule that it was self defense and drop the charges. The day you called 911, you did not hang up the phone and they have everything on tape. It won't be long baby." David said as he put his hand up to the window. I placed my hand on the window. I wished that he could hold me; I needed to feel his strong embrace.

"When you get out, you and Kacess'ion are coming to live with me. I am already in the process of having your things removed from the house. I hope you don't object," he said with a smile. I was so happy that I had a man that liked to take care of me. I really felt blessed.

"Yes that's fine. I like your house much better than mine anyway," I laughed.

"Oh and don't worry about your job, I talked with human resources, your job will still be there when you get out. It pays to know people in high places," he laughed. I started crying. I could not help myself. It seemed like so much had happened in my life.

"Don't cry baby. We are going to get through this together," he said smiling at me. The deputy came over to me and tapped me on the shoulder.

"Your time is almost up, rap it up quickly," she said and then walked away.

"I put a hundred dollars on your books and I brought you a goody bag with some panties, socks, tee shirts, and some magazines in it. The deputy said you would get it tonight. Try to relax while you are here. I promise that you will not have to be here too much longer."

"Thank you David," I said as I stood up. I replaced the phone on the hook and blew him a kiss. He smiled and mouthed the words "I love you." The deputy escorted me back to my cell.

The next week the lawyer came to see me just as David promised. The deputies allowed me to go into a special room where inmates could speak with their lawyers. My lawyer turned on a small tape recorder then asked me to tell him my story. I started back to when Clyde and I were on our honeymoon. I told him about the rapes, the beatings, and the time he had pulled a gun on me and held it to my head. I told him about the domestic violence shelter in Cleveland and about "The Love House." I told him about the break in and everything that had happened the day that I killed Clyde, including him confessing to killing his first wife, her lover, and my cousin. After I was finished with my story, he turned off the recorder. He told me that he had spoken to my uncle, my grandmother, and the women from the shelter.

He said he had enough information to take to the judge and that most likely the judge would rule on self defense and dismiss the charges without us having to go to a trial. After our meeting, I felt good. It seemed like my nightmare would soon be over.

After I left the meeting with my lawyer, I called Rita to check on Kacess'ion.

"Hello," Rita answered. I could hear a baby crying in the background.

"Hey Rita, its Karen, I just called to see how Kacess'ion is doing, sounds like you have your hands full," I chuckled.

"Little Samuel is trying to resist taking a nap, hold on while I put him back in his crib." She said then I heard her put the telephone down. Every few minutes a recorded message came on reminding me that I was an inmate. I leaned against the wall waiting for Rita to come back to the phone. Rita had really done well for herself. She was so good with kids. Parents fought to get their children into her open daycare slots. She took the kids on field trips, helped them with homework, and did arts and crafts with them. It seemed like every week Kacess'ion would come home with something that she had made at Rita's house, baskets, beaded necklaces, pictures, just all kinds of things. She was approved for a small business loan and was having a daycare center built about five minutes away from her home. The police had apprehended her ex-husband and he was in jail serving a ten year sentence. Rita had also started dating a nice man from Chicago.

"Okay, I'm back. Sorry it took me so long," Rita replied.

"That's okay, I just wanted to know how Kacess'ion is doing, has she been asking for me."

"Yes, but I just let her know that you were away taking care of business. She has been having fun. She loves helping me with the toddlers." The message came back on letting me and Rita know that the phone was about to cut off.

"Well, give her a kiss for me okay," I said.

"I will Oh yea I almost forgot to tell you that I spoke with your uncle, he told me to tell you he would be down here to see you next week." The phone cut off before I could reply.

I went back to my cell and lay down on my bunk. Right before chow time a fight broke out between two inmates. One woman said that the other woman had been in her cell and stole something from her. I watched as the two women slung each other around the room. Deputies ran into the room, sprayed the two inmates with Mace, and then put everyone on lockdown, making us stay in our cells.

There was always a fight or some type of drama happening in our zone. There was also a lot of homosexual activity. I would see the women kissing and hugging each other. I always tried to figure out who was the man and who was the woman in the relationship. You could hear them moaning at night when they thought everyone was asleep. A few of them even made homemade dildoes. One woman who shared her dildoe had a bad yeast infection. Everyone who used her dildoe became infected.

Some of the new girls who came to our zone were picked on by the bullies. No one ever bothered me. I think the only reason they did not bother me was because they had a lot of respect for my roommate. Kim had a reputation for being a good fighter, and she did not take any mess from anyone. Kim loved children and since she knew I was pregnant, I guess she felt like she had to protect me.

At night we would sit up and talk, sometimes we discussed God, she felt like God did not exist. I use to pull out the bible and talk to her, trying to convince her that not only did God exist, but that he loved her and that if she put her faith in him, he would turn her life around.

"It is chow time!" The deputy yelled. I looked down stairs and saw the trustees pulling in the meal carts. The cell doors were opened and everyone went over to the carts and stood in line as the deputies handed out trays and milk. I stood in line behind a white woman named "T," she was in jail for killing her pimp. She looked like she was a serious drug addict. She must have had connections in jail because everyone was scared of her. She never bothered me, Kim made sure of that.

When it was my turn, they handed me a tray of something that resembled Salisbury steak and mash potatoes. The food in jail was horrible, but it was much better than the sandwiches we were forced to eat in intake. I forced myself to eat because I knew that I was eating for two. After dinner, I went back to my cell and lay down. All I could think about was what the judge was going to say on the 23rd.

On my next visitation day, the guard came and escorted me to the visitation area. When I walked into the booth, I saw Uncle Jason. I had not seen him in more than five years. I could tell that he had aged a lot.

His smooth brown skin was now creased with age lines, and his hair had gray in it. I smiled at him and sat down at the booth. We both picked up the phones to talk.

"Hello Uncle Jason. Thank you for coming to see me," I said into the phone.

"You have always been like a daughter to me Karen," he said smiling.

"How was your trip? I asked.

"Oh fine, as soon as mom called me I booked a flight. I would have come sooner but I was in the middle of a trial." He said with a smile.

"How is grandmother doing?" I asked.

"She is fine; she has just been worried about you. Your father however is not doing well at all. He is in the hospital. They diagnosed him with cirrhosis of the liver and hepatitis B. He has been in and out of the hospital over the last few months. This time it is worse. They don't expect him to live much longer."

"How long has he been in the hospital this time?" I asked.

"About a week, they had to revive him twice. He is barely hanging in there." He said with a sigh.

"I'm sorry to hear that." I could tell by the expression on my uncle's face that he was disappointed that I was not showing more concern.

"Uncle Jason, the day that I killed Clyde, he confessed to killing Linda, he also let me know that he killed his first wife and her lover." I said slowly. My uncle surprised me by slamming his hand forcefully against the table.

"That sick bastard killed my baby!" He yelled with a shocked look on his face. I felt so bad. I knew that Linda's death really hurt him. Linda had been his pride and joy.

"To think he came to the funeral acting like he was so concerned and wanted to help find the killer. Well I am glad that you did kill him, if I had known I would have killed him myself!" Tears started rolling down his cheeks.

"I'm so sorry Uncle Jason!" I started crying. It was a few minutes before either of us could speak.

"My lawyer told me that he is going to present all the evidence to the judge, showing him that it was self defense. My court date is in two weeks. He said that my case would probably be dismissed, and I would not have to go to trial."

"I will make sure that I am there," he replied.

We talked for a little longer. He gave me a rundown on how the rest of our family had been doing. When my time was up, he stood up, blew me a kiss, and told me to stay strong. I watched him walk away from the booth with slouched shoulders. I knew the news of his daughters' murderer was weighing heavy on his heart.

LEARNING TO FORGIVE

PART VI

In a world of imperfection,

In a world of sin.

No one is perfect and everyone sins.

We must learn to forgive each other.

We must learn to love one another.

Only forgiveness will set our spirits free.

I will forgive you, and you will forgive me.

This is how God intended it to be.

CHAPTER 23

Two weeks after my uncle came to see me, I went to court. This court appearance would decide whether they would charge me and have a trial or dismiss the case and let me go. I was so nervous. I could not sleep the night before. My roommate surprised me by asking to pray with me before I left to go to court.

When I got to the courtroom, I saw all my friends, my uncle, Mrs. Francis, and David sitting in the audience. The prosecutor was the first to speak. He tried to make me look like a heartless criminal who had gotten great pleasure out of killing her husband. When the prosecutor finished his speech, I felt like I was going to throw up. Then my lawyer presented my side of the case and gave the judge all the evidence that he had collected over the last few weeks.

After hearing both sides the judge called a break and went back to his chamber to deliberate over the evidence. When court resumed, he ruled that from the evidence it was obvious that the murder had been self-defense and dismissed all the charges. Everyone in the courtroom applauded the decision. I started crying and yelling "Thank You Jesus!" My nightmare was finally over.

The night before I was to be released, the Chaplin called me into his office and informed me that my father had passed away. I went back to my cell and cried. I never expected to feel sad about his passing. In order to start my life over I knew that I needed to forgive my father and Helen for what they had done to me as a child. God says that we must forgive each other. Holding anger in your heart only wounds the soul and stunts spiritual growth.

When they released me the next day, David was in the waiting room ready to take me home.

"It's over baby," he said as I ran up to him. He picked me up in his arms, twirled me around, and then gave me a passionate kiss right there in front of all the deputies.

"You guys need to take that home!" The police officer demanded. We laughed and walked out of the jail. It felt so good to be out of that place. When we arrived at his house, I noticed that there were a large number of cars in the parking lot. When I walked into the house, everyone yelled, "Surprise!" There was a big banner going across David's living room that read 'Welcome Home'. Kacess'ion ran up to me and gave me a gift that she had made at Rita's house. I saw Monica, Rita, Jessica and their families, Ms. Francis and her family, my lawyer and his family, all our friends from work and women from the shelter. We had a house full of people; David had a large buffet table with all kinds of foods and drinks on it. It felt so good to be home.

That night I received a call from Uncle Jason. He had to catch a flight back to Ohio and was not able to come to my party.

"Welcome home Karen," he said.

"Thank you," I replied.

"Did the Chaplin tell you about your father?" He asked.

"Yes, he told me last night."

"Are you going to come to the funeral?" I hesitated before answering, a long time ago, I had vowed never to return to Ohio, but I knew that I needed to go back so that I could finally close the chapter on that portion of my life.

"Yes, I will come."

"Good, don't worry about money, I will call and book you a flight," he stated before hanging up. That night as I laid in David's arms I thought about my trip back to Ohio. David had offered to take time off work and go with me, but I told him that this was something I needed to do by myself. I knew that there was one person that I needed to see while I was in Columbus. My uncle called back later that night and gave me the information for my flight. He told me that the flight would be leaving the next day at 8:30 in the morning. He told me that I needed to go to the Delta airlines booth, show them my ID and pick up my plane ticket. We talked for a few more minutes before we hung up the telephone.

"Are you sure you don't want me to go with you?" David asked. He had been there for me throughout my whole ordeal. It felt so good to know that I was loved. If I had never taken that step of faith and left Clyde, I would not have met the man that God had for me.

"No honey, I need to do this by myself," I said as I kissed him.

That night David wanted to make love, but I told him that it was wrong for us to have sex out of wedlock. I let him know that I made a lot of promises to God while I was in jail and I planned to honor them.

There was nothing I could do to change the fact that I was pregnant, but from this day forward I decided I wanted to try to live right. I could tell he was not too pleased with my decision. For the first time since David and I had started dating, we did not make love, instead he held me in his arms until I fell asleep.

The next morning David drove me to Rita's house to drop Kacess'ion off then he took me to the airport.

"If you need me, don't hesitate to call," he said kissing me softly on my lips. I loved the feel of his lips on mine.

"David, I want you to know that I love you very much," I said as I held his hand. He lifted my hand to his mouth and kissed it. We got out of the car and walked to the Delta information office holding hands. I handed the clerk my drivers' license. She looked up my name in the computer then handed me my ticket and checked in my luggage, then David and I walked to the terminal still holding each other's hands. I handed my ticket to the man standing behind the booth.

"Here you go Ms. King," he said as he handed me my stub. I hated hearing the name King. David must have been reading my mind, because he took both my hands in his and pulled me toward him, looking deeply into my eyes.

"I don't like the last name King. I think Smith would sound so much better," he said smiling. Then he surprised me by getting down on one knee in front of everyone. I looked at him and put my hand over my mouth to contain my scream. I glanced at all the people who were watching us.

"Honey you are making people stare at us," I said blushing with embarrassment.

"I don't care who is watching us. Karen, would you please do me the honor of being my wife?" He asked as he reached into his pocket and pulled out a little black box. He opened it and showed me a diamond ring that was so big and shinny it made me gasp.

"Yes baby. I would be honored to be your wife," I said as tears began rolling down my cheeks. He pulled the ring out of the box and slid it onto my finger.

"I want you to know that I am not marrying you because you said that we can't have sex or because you are pregnant with my child. I am marrying you because I love you. I fell in love with you the first day we met, when you bumped into me at the Hyatt and spilt your drink on me. I cannot imagine spending the rest of my life without you by my side." He stood up and pulled me into his arms giving me a passionate kiss. People who were standing close to us started clapping and congratulating us on our engagement.

"Ms. King, your plane is boarding," the flight attendant said as he tapped me softly on the shoulder.

"I have to go baby," I said as I kissed him on his cheek.

"Hurry home," he said as he released me.

I got onto the plane and found my assigned seat. I sat down and stared at the large diamond on my finger.

"Thank you God for sending me true love," I whispered. I laid my head back against the chair and looked out the window as the airplane began ascending into the clouds. I had mixed emotions about the trip back to Columbus. I had not been there in almost six years. I knew that everyone in my family knew I killed Clyde. My uncle told me that the funeral was going to be tomorrow night. I knew everyone in my family was going to be there.

I wondered what thoughts would race through their heads when they saw me. I decided that before I went to my grandmother's house I was going to pay Helen a visit.

Once the plane landed, I went to claim my luggage. My uncle told me he had to be in court and would not be able to meet me at the airport. He said that he paid for a rental car. I went over to the rental car office and signed for the car that my uncle had reserved. The baggage boy began loading the trunk with my suitcases, after he was finished I gave him a handsome tip. "Thanks," he said with a big grin on his face.

It was a very cloudy and gloomy day in Columbus, as I got into the car I turned on the radio and searched for the R&B station that I use to listen to. The weather broadcaster stated that there was a 30% chance of showers today. I turned the key in the ignition and drove the rental car out of the airport and onto Stelzer Road. I glanced out the window at my surroundings, as I crossed over Broad Street I saw a large crowd of people standing at the Cota bus stop. It reminded me of the days when I use to catch the bus. As I made a left turn onto Livingston Avenue, I noticed that most of the stores were still open; the street still looked the same. My uncle told me that my dad and Helen never moved from the apartment that they lived in when I was young. As I drove down

Livingston Avenue, I noticed how the neighborhood gradually changed from middle class to the slums.

I saw an old man sitting on a chair in front of a barbershop with a liqueur bottle in his hand and half-dressed young girls walking up and down the street glancing at every passing car. Teenage mothers were pushing their babies in strollers and young guys were standing on the corner in front of abandoned houses, waiting for cars to stop so that they could sell drugs. Not much had changed on Livingston Avenue in the last six years.

I pulled out in front of Helen's rundown apartment building. I stepped out of the car, locked the door, and took a deep breath as I walked down the long walkway toward her apartment. I thought back to the day when I first moved in with my father and Helen after Grandma Ellis had died. As I entered her building I passed by two young men sitting on the sidewalk, they had red scarves tied around their heads and there was alot of money on the ground. They were playing a game of dice. There was a funny smell in the air, I knew that they were not smoking cigars. I knew they were smoking blunts packed with marijuana.

I walked up the steps and knocked on Helen's front door.

"Who is it?" A young woman's voice yelled from inside.

"Its Karen King, is Helen White home?" I yelled back. I heard a loud noise and then the door slowly opened. I immediately recognized my half sister, although I had not seen her since she was a little girl her features still looked the same. Only her height and body size had changed, she was no longer the skinny little girl that I remembered. She was now a tall and obese teenager.

"Come in," she said holding the door wide open. When I walked into the apartment I felt like I was taking a step back into the past, although some of the furniture was new, most of the things that were in the apartment were the same as when I had lived there. They still had the same floor model television, and the new furniture was in the same location that the old furniture had been.

"Momma, Karen is here to see you!" She yelled as she plopped onto the couch and continued eating her gallon of strawberry ice cream.

I looked at the walls and saw pictures of my little brother. I had not seen him since he was a baby; he looked just like my father. When Helen walked into the living room a look of surprise covered her face.

"Karen, you came back," she said as she sat down in a chair next to the couch.

"Yes, I came back for my father's funeral. I stopped over here because I wanted to ask you a question."

"Please, sit down," Helen said gesturing to the red and blue love seat that was next to the front door.

"No thanks, I will not be staying here long."

"Well, what's your question?" She asked as she reached and picked up her box of cigarettes off the coffee table and lit one, taking a long drag and blowing the smoke out of her nose and mouth. It's funny, she had not changed at all; she was still a big woman, she still wore a lot of makeup, and still wore her big fluffy wigs.

"I just wanted to know what I did to you to make you hate me so much." Her face went pale as if she had seen a ghost.

"I have never hated you. I love you like a daughter," she said in a low voice as she took another puff from her cigarette before placing it in the ashtray.

"You never showed me love. You must have hated me, no one treats a person the way you treated me unless he hates the person. You and my father tortured an innocent child." I stated in a low voice. She surprised me when she started crying, for years I saw her as a cold woman without feelings or emotions.

"Your father and I were going through a lot of problems back then. I guess I was just not ready for a ready-made family," she sobbed. My sister did not say anything. She just looked at me I wondered if she even remembered the abuse. She was only three or four at the time.

"You tried to kill me. You tried to destroy my spirit. You knew that my father was molesting me and you never tried to stop him, instead you joined him in torturing me. It has taken me a long time to get over the abuse that I experienced, but with God's help I have learned to forgive you and this has healed me from my pain. I just wanted to come back here and let you know that I forgive you. I do not hate you Helen. I do however feel sorry for you, anyone who treats a child the way you treated me must have mental problems." I said as I walked toward the front door.

"I am so sorry," she sobbed as she lowered her head and covered her face with her hands. "I pray that you get some professional counseling Helen." I said as I opened the front door. "I will see you at my father's funeral tomorrow." Then I turned and walked out the door, closing it behind me. Somehow, I did not feel like I had just won a big battle against the wicked witch of the north; instead, I really did feel sorry for Helen. I knew she had been carrying around the guilt of what she had done.

I realized that forgiving her really didn't have anything to do with her. Whether I forgave her or not her life would go on. My forgiving her had everything to do with allowing myself to get over what had happened and to heal emotionally, so that I could move on with my life. As long as I hold bitterness in my heart, the only person I am really hurting is myself. I felt like I had finally gained closure. I walked back to my car and drove to my grandmothers' house.

My grandmother and I had a long talk; she let me know how much she missed me. It felt good to see her again.

The next day I went to my father's funeral. All of my family was there. I walked up to the casket and looked down at the man I had known as my father, the man who molested me and had allowed his wife to torture his first-born child. I started crying.

"I forgive you daddy," I said as I touched his cold hard hands.

After the burial I checked into a hotel, I was ready to go home to my future husband and my daughter.

On the plane ride home I thought about the things that had happened in my life. I had experienced a lot of hardship, jumped hurdles, and experienced a lot of pain. I do not understand why I had to go through such a hard life, but the one thing I did know was that all my trials and tribulations had made me a much stronger person.

It had made me a survivor.

CHAPTER 24

JULY 15, 2004

It has been almost seventeen years since I was released from jail. David and I were married six months after I was released from jail. I had a beautiful wedding at my husband's church; we flew to Paris for our honeymoon. I felt like Cinderella. I now have two beautiful daughters, Kacess'ion Monique age 22 and Linda Marie age 16. Kacess'ion has grown into a beautiful young lady. She is currently in a female singing group called Lady's Delight. I hope her group becomes very successful. My other daughter, Linda Marie reminds me of my cousin Linda. I have to really keep an eye on her because she is very stubborn, headstrong, and hot in the pants. I worry about her a lot.

I help my husband with his practice and I work PRN in the ER at Grady hospital. I also work at "The Love House." Ms. Francis retired, so I took her place as mother of the house. I really enjoy my job; however, some of the women that come through 'The Love House' really get on my nerves. A few of them have some serious problems that have nothing to do with domestic violence, but there are a few, like a young girl I met in the E.R. named Tabitha, who really touches my heart. Tabitha is only nineteen years old; she has been turning tricks since she was fourteen. The day she came into the E.R. her pimp had beaten her so badly that you could hardly see her features.

However, that's another story.

I am truly happy and at peace; I think about the prayer that I prayed to God so many years earlier, when I found out that I was pregnant with Kacess'ion.

The pastor was right, God does hear you when you pray, I took a great leap of faith and trusted him, and because of that faith, he blessed me with far more than I had asked for. His word is true. . .

WORDS FROM THE AUTHOR

This is a fictional story and the characters do not exist. However, the abuse that Karen King experienced as a child was taken from my own true-life experience. I decided to tell the story of my abuse in hopes that people will realize that child abuse is a very serious situation that should no longer be ignored.

Millions of women and children experience some type of domestic violence every day. If you are a woman being abused, leave the situation. God will provide for you. All you have to do is take a step of faith and believe. You may say "oh, but my situation is not as bad as some of the characters in this book." I want you to know that if you are being abused in any way, you are experiencing domestic violence. The abuse may be verbal instead of physical.

If you suspect that, a child is being molested or abused. Please do not ignore it. Too many children are killed every day because no one took action. When a child is being abused, there are warning signs. Please do not ignore these signs, do not turn your back and say "I don't want to get involved." It may be your call that saves that child's life, or helps get the child out of an unhealthy situation.

In my own situation, when I became an adult, I ran into people that lived near my father and my stepmother. They told me that they knew I was being abused, and apologized for not trying to stop it. I accept all of their apologies; I thank God that I was not one of the unlucky children who do not survive their abuse.

If my book can help at least one woman leave her abuser, or aide in rescuing at least one child from a violent home, or assist one person in taking a step of faith and trusting God, then I believe this book will have fulfilled its purpose. This book does not follow the norm of a Christian book, but please do not allow that to stop you from receiving the message.

It is my prayer that this book will cross over all socioeconomic boundaries. Domestic violence is experienced by people of all different races, nationalities, and backgrounds; it is experienced by rich, middle class and poor people. My goal is to bring about awareness through my books.

If you are a victim of domestic violence and need assistance please call: National Domestic Violence Hotline: 1-800-799-7233

If you suspect that a child is being abused please call the police or call National Child Abuse Hotlines: 1-800-CHILDREN or 1-800-4-A-CHILD

Being a victim of child abuse and defining that as love made it easier for me to accept abuse in my adult relationships and also made it more difficult to leave. On my road to healing I became connected with Safe Haven, a transitional program for victims of domestic violence. Due to the decrease in government funding, it is crucial that the private sector supports organizations such as Safe Haven in order for them to continue to exist. I would like to ask all those who read this novel and would like to help, or need a write off for tax purposes, Please send a donation to: Safe Haven Transitional Inc., P.O. Box 501 Conley, Ga 30288. Or call 404-241-8740

Watch for the sequel to THIS CAN'T BE LOVE:
'THE LOVE HOUSE' ......COMING SOON

If you would like to be added to the mailing list for 'The Love House', or Essence....The poetry of life Part II when it's released, or if you have any comments about the book, or questions about domestic violence, please Email me at ebony142@hotmail.com

GOD BLESS,

Patricia Goins

ESSENCE
THE POETRY OF LIFE

Is a collection of poetic words of wisdom and life experiences intended to nourish your spirit, God has inspired me to include a prophetic word to be received by those who read this book.

LOVE
OR
LUST

LOVE OR LUST, WAS IT WRONG TO RUSH?
SHOULD WE HAVE TAKEN IT SLOW?
I GUESS NOW WE WILL NEVER KNOW.

I STILL REMEMBER THE FIRST TIME WE MET.
IT IS A DAY I SHALL NEVER FORGET.
YOU WERE SO FLY YOU CAUGHT MY EYE.
YOU WERE SO REAL; I COULD NOT DENY YOUR SEX APPEAL.
YOU KNEW JUST WHAT TO SAY, TO MAKE ME COME YOUR WAY.

WHEN YOU TOOK ME OUT, WE HAD SO MUCH FUN.
WHEN WE DANCED, OUR BODIES SEEMED TO BECOME ONE.
YOU WHISPERED SWEET WORDS OF LOVE IN MY EAR.
IT FELT SO RIGHT TO LET YOU SPEND THE NIGHT.
WHEN WE MADE LOVE, I FELT ON TOP OF THE MOON.
NOW I WONDER IF I SHARED MY BODY WITH YOU TOO SOON.

HOW COULD SOMETHING THAT SEEMED SO RIGHT, CHANGE OVERNIGHT.

NOW WHEN I CALL, YOU TREAT ME LIKE A CASUAL FRIEND.
I WONDER IF THERE IS ANOTHER WOMAN ON THE OTHER END.
YOU ACT LIKE OUR LOVE DID NOT MEAN A THING.
SOMETIMES YOU WILL NOT EVEN ANSWER THE PHONE WHEN I RING.

HOW COULD SOMETHING THAT SEEMED SO RIGHT, CHANGE OVERNIGHT.

SECRETS

YOU AND I HAVE BEEN PLAYMATES SINCE WE WERE ONE; OUR MOTHERS HAVE BEEN CLOSE SINCE THEY WERE YOUNG.

WE USE TO PUT ON MAKEUP, PLAY DRESS UP, AND PLAY SCHOOL WHEN WE WERE SIX, THEN RUN OUTSIDE, PLAY HOPSCOTCH AND COLLECT FUNNY LOOKING STICKS.

AS TEENAGERS WE BECAME BEST FRIENDS, GOING OUT ON DOUBLE DATES AND TO THE DRIVE END.

WHEN WE BECAME YOUNG ADULTS WE WOULD GO OUT TO THE CLUBS AND DANCE TIL DAWN, THEN GO HOME AND LAUGH ABOUT THE NUMBERS WE HAD COLLECTED AND THE THINGS WE HAD DONE.

SO I UNDERSTAND WHY YOU FELT SAFE SHARING YOUR SPECIAL SECRET WITH ME, A SECRET THAT YOU COULD NOT SHARE WITH YOUR OWN FAMILY. I MUST ADMIT YOU SURPRISED ME WHEN YOU REVEALED THAT YOU HAD NO INTREST IN MEN, AND THAT SINCE YOU WERE YOUNG YOU HAVE ONLY BEEN ATTRACTED TO OTHER WOMEN.

YOU SAY YOU HAVE BEEN CARRYING THIS SECRET ALL YOUR LIFE, BUT YOU DIDN'T WANT TO TELL ANYONE

BECAUSE YOU DIDN'T WANT TO BE JUDGED FOR DOING WHAT SOCIETY SAYS IS NOT RIGHT.

YOU ALSO REVEALED THAT YOU ARE HAVING AN AFFAIR WITH ANOTHER MAN'S WIFE.

I CANNOT JUDGE YOU FOR WHAT YOU DO; AFTER ALL I HAVE DEMONS THAT I DEAL WITH TOO.

IT REALLY DOES NOT MATTER WHAT OTHER PEOPLE THINK OR SAY

THIS IS YOUR LIFE AND YOU MUST LIVE IT YOUR WAY.

ALL I CAN SAY IS TO GO TO THE LORD IN PRAYER; YOU WILL FIND ALL OF YOUR ANSWERS THERE.

TO READ MORE OF ESSENCE...THE POETRY OF LIFE, JUST LOG ONTO:

www.iuniverse.com, www.amazon.com, or www.barnesandnoble.com AND ORDER IT FROM THE ONLINE BOOK STORE. If you would like to find out how to become a self published author please Log onto: www.msnusers.com/how to publish your book

THANK YOU
&
GOD BLESS

ABOUT THE AUTHOR

Patricia Goins is a nurse, a poet, and an advocate against domestic violence. She currently resides in Riverdale, Georgia with her four children.